KEY HUNTERS

THE SPY'S SECRET

by Eric Luper

Illustrated by Lisa K. Weber

SCHOLASTIC INC.

KEY HUNTERS

*Getting lost in a good book
has never been this dangerous!*

CHAPTER 1

"Ugh, why does Mrs. Cabanos always give us boring crossword puzzles for homework?" Cleo asked Evan across the library table. "What's a four-letter word for 'fake butter'?"

Evan didn't look up from his math. "Oleo," he said.

"What about a three-letter word for 'anger'?"

"Ire."

" 'Sea eagle'?"

1

"Erne."

"Jai—"

"Alai."

Cleo dropped her pencil. "How do you know all this stuff?"

Evan shrugged. "My parents do the cross-word every weekend."

"I read the comics every weekend," Cleo said. "How come we don't get homework about that?"

"Don't you get a great feeling when you finish a puzzle?" Evan asked. "Like you can accomplish anything?"

Cleo shook her head. "Puzzles give me headaches. Anyhow, no one says that."

"Says what?"

Cleo made a serious face and sat tall in her seat. " 'Honey, would you please pass the *oleo*? I'd like to spread it on my toast.' "

2

Evan laughed. "I don't think it's a word people use anymore."

"Then what's the point of giving us homework about it?"

"I have no idea," Evan said.

"I . . . have . . . no . . . idea!" a voice said mockingly. It was Ms. Crowley, their not-so-nice librarian. She walked up behind Evan.

A few days earlier, Ms. Crowley had led them to the magical library hidden under their school. It was she who showed them that any book they opened would sweep them off to the world inside that book. It was because of her that Evan and Cleo felt they might find their first librarian, Ms. Hilliard, who had mysteriously disappeared into one of those books.

Each word Ms. Crowley said was punctuated by the sharp click of her pointy, uncomfortable-looking high heels. "What do you 'have no idea' about?"

"I just said 'oleo' isn't a word people use anymore," Evan said. "People say 'margarine.'"

"Or they don't say it at all," Cleo said. "Margarine is bad for you."

Ms. Crowley circled their table like a hungry wolf. "Maybe *I* use the word 'oleo,'" she said. "Why don't you ask me?"

"Umm . . . okay," Evan said. "Ms. Crowley, do you ever say 'oleo'?"

"This is a quiet study period!" she barked. "Two days of detention for both of you!"

"But . . ." Cleo said.

"Quiet!" Ms. Crowley barked again. "Now it's four days!"

Evan raised his hand.

"Yes?" Ms. Crowley said.

"I was just wondering . . ."

"I told you to be quiet," Ms. Crowley said. "That's eight days!"

"But I—"

"Sixteen days!" She bent down so her face was close to Evan's. "Do you want to try for thirty-two?"

Evan began to open his mouth, but closed it again.

"That's better," Ms. Crowley said. "Now, there may be something you could do to get me to forget about all this detention. One of you holds a key that unlocks a certain book. If you gave me that key, I might forget about your sixty-four days of detention."

"Sixty-four?" Cleo burst out. "It was sixteen!"

"Now it's one hundred and twenty-eight!" Ms. Crowley bellowed. "Won't Principal Flynn

5

be disappointed in her star pupil and her star athlete? Won't your parents be upset?"

"I . . . I . . ." Evan's hand moved to his pocket. He felt the lump made by the key they had gotten at the end of their last adventure.

Cleo stood. "I left it at home."

Ms. Crowley smiled a toothy grin. "Be sure to bring it tomorrow," she said. "A strange underground library is no place for children."

Ms. Crowley clicked back to the front desk and began stamping books loudly.

Evan wiggled his fingers into his pocket. The key was warm from pressing against his leg all day. He pulled it out by its chain and held it up. As it spun, the key glinted in the light from the window.

Cleo snatched it and darted between the bookshelves.

"Wait!" Evan hissed.

"Wait!" Ms. Crowley called after them.

Evan chased Cleo through the maze of shelves until they reached the nonfiction section. Cleo scampered up the bookcase, stretched as high as she could, and grabbed hold of the huge, dusty, boring-looking book titled *Literature: Elements and Genre from Antiquity to Modern-Day.*

The book tipped forward. The secret bookcase swung open.

Evan followed Cleo down the stairs into the magical room beneath their elementary school. Even though he'd seen it before, the library amazed him. The shelves, sliding ladders, and spiral staircases were made of dark wood and stretched into darkness above them. Catwalks and balconies reached around corners and across gaps to let readers explore every nook. At the back of the library, over a stone fireplace, hung a tapestry that showed an image of an open book with people swirling into it among a sea of colorful letters.

The fire in the fireplace burst to life, sending out a warm glow.

"We have to hurry," Cleo said. "Ms. Crowley is right behind us."

"There are thousands of books in this library," Evan said. "How do we know which one to choose?"

"Any of them," Cleo said. She grabbed a book off the shelf. The title read *The Jumpy Puppy*. The cover had a picture of a brown puppy sitting in its water bowl. "Let's go here. There's nothing scary or dangerous about jumpy puppies."

"Jumpy puppies aren't potty trained," Evan said.

"That's simple compared to a chandelier almost falling on our heads like in *The Case of the Mysterious Moonstone*."

"Good point," Evan said.

Cleo jiggled the key against the tiny keyhole. "It doesn't fit."

Evan heard a metallic clank. A rolling ladder with brass rungs slid along a track and stopped in front of them.

"I guess we go up," Evan said.

Cleo grabbed the first rung and started to climb. Evan followed. As they reached the top of the ladder, sharp heels sounded on the stone floor below.

"Come down this instant!" Ms. Crowley hollered.

"Hurry!" Cleo ran along a metal catwalk that wrapped around several walls of bookshelves.

Evan followed her. "Where are we going?" he asked.

"Away from Ms. Crowley!"

They reached the end of the catwalk. Evan felt dizzy. The ground was thirty feet below them, and he hated heights. Cleo grabbed a rope that was tied to the railing. It stretched into the darkness above them. She stuffed it into Evan's hands.

"Hold on tight!" she said.

"What are you do—"

But before Evan could finish his sentence, Cleo had flung them out into open space. Air whooshed past Evan's ears. His stomach flip-flopped. They swung across the library and landed on another balcony.

"There!" Cleo pointed to a small desk. A lamp shone on a blue book with a silver lock on the cover. The title read *The Viper's Secret*.

"That's it," she said.

Evan's heart was still pounding in his chest. "How do you know?"

"The key matches the lock."

"Lots of things are silver," Evan said.

Cleo ignored him and slid the key into the lock. It fit perfectly.

"Stop!" Ms. Crowley screamed from the catwalk behind them. The rope was swinging back and forth. Ms. Crowley reached for it each time it came close. "Don't turn that key!"

Cleo grinned. "I'd never disobey my school librarian," she said.

She held the key tight and spun *The Viper's Secret* on the desk. The lock popped open. Letters burst from the pages of the book like a thousand crazy spiders. The letters tumbled in the air around them and began to spell words. The words turned into sentences, the sentences paragraphs. Before long, they could barely see through the letter confetti.

Then everything went black.

CHAPTER 2

Water sprayed against Evan's face. He breathed the salty air and held tight to Cleo's waist as they jetted across a crowded harbor. They were on a Jet Ski, and Cleo was at the helm. They wore matching wet suits, each with a gold diamond on the chest.

"Where are we?" Evan called over the roar of the engine.

"No idea," Cleo said over her shoulder. "But I've always wanted to drive one of these things." She weaved around several boats. Water splashed into the air.

·Evan heard a roar behind them. He glanced back to see a red speedboat. The men onboard were wearing dark face masks. These weren't the sort of face masks for deep-sea diving; they were the sort for bank robbing.

"Does this thing go faster?" Evan asked.

"I've got it at half speed," she said.

"Try three-quarters," Evan said. He glanced behind them again and saw the masked men pointing at them.

"Who are they?" Cleo cried out.

"We don't have time to ask their names," Evan said. "And they don't exactly look friendly anyway."

Cleo twisted her wrist and the Jet Ski shot forward. But within seconds, the boat caught up.

Evan reached around Cleo and pressed a button on the handlebars that looked like a puffy cloud. White smoke poofed out behind them.

"Turn right!" Evan shouted.

Cleo yanked the handlebars. They shot between two small fishing boats.

The red boat darted through the cloud and circled around until they were once again on Cleo and Evan's tail.

"That only slowed them down for a second," Cleo said.

"What should we do?" Evan said.

Cleo leaned forward and hit the throttle. The Jet Ski pounded against the water, and they sped even faster. Evan almost slipped off the seat, but somehow he managed to hold on.

The red boat was still gaining on them.

"I have a plan!" Cleo said.

"I hope your plan includes not getting run over by a boat filled with thugs!" Evan said.

Then he saw it. Cleo was driving straight toward a low bridge that connected two parts of the harbor. The path underneath it looked narrow. Maybe too narrow.

"We're not going to make it," Evan said.

"Sure we will!" Cleo said.

The red boat had almost caught up to them. They could hear one of the thugs over the boat's deafening motor. "We have you now, Agent Cleo and Agent Evan!"

"Faster!" Evan screamed.

"This is as fast as it goes!" Cleo cried.

Evan reached around Cleo and pressed another button. This one looked like a tiny flame.

The engine roared and the Jet Ski rocketed

forward through the narrow path under the bridge. The masked men barely had time to leap clear before their boat slammed into the bridge and exploded. Flames burst toward them, licking at their backs.

Evan and Cleo circled around to see the masked men bobbing in the water.

"Hmm," Cleo said.

"What's wrong?" Evan asked.

"We must be spies, right? Aren't we supposed to say something clever right now?"

Evan thought for a moment. "How about, 'Nice day for a swim.'"

Cleo shook her head.

Evan felt a buzzing against his thigh. He fished a phone out of his pocket. The screen read AVERY PHILLIPS. A man's head appeared.

"Agent Evan," the man said. "Are you and Agent Cleo fooling with the agency's Jet

Ski?" Before Evan could answer, the man said, "Well, enough of that. Return to base at once."

"Where *is* base?" Evan asked.

"You're spies," the man said. "Figure it out."

"Okay . . ."

"You're supposed to say 'roger,'" Avery said.

"Who's Roger?"

Avery sighed. "Roger means you've received the message."

"Ummmm . . . roger?"

"Then you're supposed to say 'wilco,'" Avery added. "That means you'll do what I've asked."

"Roger," Evan said again.

"And wilco?" Avery said.

"Roger and wilco," Evan said.

Avery shook his head. The screen went black.

"So where are we going?" Cleo asked as they puttered along the edge of the harbor.

"There," Evan said, pointing to a battered garage door. The building looked like it hadn't seen a coat of paint in a century.

"What makes you think so?"

Evan traced the gold diamond on his wet suit, then pointed. Above the weathered garage door hung a crooked sign with a gold diamond painted on it.

Cleo steered the Jet Ski toward it. As they approached, the door opened. Floodlights powered on and a man in a crisp suit and tie helped them onto the dock. Evan recognized him as Avery Phillips. Avery held out a dollar bill. It had been torn in half.

"I'm sorry," Evan said. "I don't accept tips."

"Especially torn-up dollars," Cleo added. "What are we going to buy with that?"

Avery smiled. "Please check your pocket."

Evan tucked his hand into his pocket and pulled out a torn dollar bill. Avery held it alongside his own. They fit perfectly, like puzzle pieces.

"You can never be too careful," Avery said. "There are imposters everywhere. Agents Evan and Cleo, welcome to A.C.R.O.N.Y.M."

"A.C.R.O.N.Y.M.?" Cleo said.

"Agency for the Capture and Research Of Nefarious Masterminds," Avery said.

"There's no 'Y,'" Evan said.

"Pardon me?" Avery said.

"An acronym is when you put together the first letter of a bunch of words to spell another," he explained. "You're missing a 'Y' word."

Avery stiffened. "Well, we can't all be perfect acronym makers, can we? Now, please follow me."

He led them to an old wooden door and began pressing different nail heads. Then he pushed on one of the hinges and the door swung open. "It may not look like it, but this is high-tech security at work. If you don't get the sequence right, you're in for a nasty shock."

He motioned for them to enter and pulled the door shut behind them. This room was nothing like the beat-up garage they had just left. A huge screen covered the back wall. Agents in suits sat hunched over computer terminals. In the far corner, a man wearing a black jumpsuit led a group through some tough-looking martial arts moves.

"This is seriously cool," Evan whispered.

"Seriously," Cleo said.

Avery smiled. "Welcome to the secret base of A.C.R.O.N.Y.M."

CHAPTER 3

Avery leaned back in his desk chair. "We have a problem," he said. "Our top spy, Samuel Dearth, has been captured. I need you to rescue him."

Avery pressed a few buttons on a computer tablet. An image of a man with perfect teeth and slicked-back golden hair appeared on the screen. His height, weight, and other details began scrolling next to him.

"Why us?" Evan asked.

"You're the only field agents in the area," Avery said. "If we wait too long, the Viper could move Agent Dearth anywhere."

"Who's the Viper?" Evan and Cleo said at once.

Avery sighed. "Don't either of you read our agency briefings? The Viper is a mysterious new criminal mastermind. He is responsible for robbing Fort Knox of its gold, stealing priceless artwork from museums around the world, and hacking into high-security government computers."

Avery tapped his tablet. An outline of a man with a question mark across his face appeared.

"That's one weird-looking dude," Evan said.

"No one has ever gotten a photo of the Viper," Avery said. "Our satellites have found

26

the location of his secret underwater base, and luckily for us, it's nearby. Now, let's get you two equipped with a few gadgets and get you on your way before the Viper—and Agent Dearth—disappear."

The gadget room was a long lab filled with high-tech instruments and scientists in white coats and goggles.

"We create all sorts of useful tools here," Avery said. "They'll help you sneak into the Viper's hideout, rescue Agent Dearth, and escape with minimal harm done."

"*Minimal* harm?" Cleo said.

Avery waved to a man with messy hair. "I'd like you to meet Dr. Omega, PhD. He runs the lab and is our top gadgeteer."

"I prefer ultra-scientist," Dr. Omega said, limping over. "I've developed a few gadgets that should come in handy for your mission." Dr. Omega tossed a watch to Evan.

"My mom makes my dad wear one of these," he said. "It counts his footsteps and keeps track of what food he eats."

"This one is different," Dr. Omega said. "Press the button on the side."

Evan pressed it. A green laser shot out of the watch, right past Avery's head. It hit the wall behind him and burned a hole.

"Sizzling," Evan said.

"That's a better spy line," Cleo said.

"That laser will cut through solid steel," Dr. Omega said. Then he unlocked a safe and took out a black device no larger than an eraser. He handed it to Cleo.

"What's this?" she asked.

"It's an electronic lock pick," Dr. Omega said. "Hold it to any lock and it will send out a huge magnetic blast that will open the lock."

"Thanks, I guess." Cleo tossed the lock pick into the air and caught it.

"Please be careful," Dr. Omega said nervously. "It's very delicate."

"It's sort of lame," Cleo said. "Don't we get harpoon guns or something?"

Avery chuckled. "You won't need harpoon guns."

Cleo tucked the lock pick into her pocket and Evan strapped the watch to his wrist as Dr. Omega led them to a railing at the back of the lab. A small submarine floated below them in a dark pool. The open hatch stuck out above the surface.

"You'll take this mini-sub to the Viper's underwater base," Avery explained. "We've found a hatch where you can attach the mini-sub while you rescue Agent Dearth. But be careful! The Viper's base is so deep that our communications signal can't reach. You'll be on your own."

Evan felt like a spy should say something brave right now. "It's not like we haven't tackled challenges like this before," he said.

"Actually, you haven't," Avery said. "This is your first real mission."

"I, uh, mean that I've *read about* missions like this," Evan said.

"Yeah," Cleo added. "In spy school."

"Yes, of course," Avery said, helping them climb into the mini-sub. He knelt down and began to swing the hatch closed. "Oh, and remember," he said. "If you two are caught, A.C.R.O.N.Y.M. will deny all knowledge of this operation."

Evan popped his head up. "Wait," he said. "You'll send agents after us, right?"

Avery cleared his throat. "I'm afraid that may not be possible."

The hatch closed tight and Evan watched through the porthole as the mini-sub sank into the dark water.

CHAPTER 4

The spotlight on the mini-sub barely lit the murky water ahead of them. All sorts of buttons and colorful lights covered the control panels. A small blip on a green screen blinked as a bright line swept around in a circle. *Ping! Ping! Ping!*

"Sonar," Evan said. "The sub is looking around even though we can't see anything."

"I hope it sees well enough," Cleo said. "I'd hate to bang right into the Viper's hideout."

After what seemed like hours, the sonar made a strange beeping noise. A peanut-shaped shadow appeared on the screen.

"Who'd have thought we'd find a giant peanut deep under the ocean?" Cleo said.

Evan pressed his face to the porthole. He could just make out two huge, dark windows. And were those . . . jagged white teeth? "That's not a peanut," he said. "The Viper's secret base is shaped like a skull!"

"I'd rather it was a peanut," Cleo said.

"I'm allergic to peanuts," Evan said. "Let's stick with skulls."

The mini-sub moved closer to the base until they felt themselves bump against it. "Automatic docking procedure initiating," a computer voice said.

"Well, that's good," Cleo said. "I don't know the first thing about docking."

But then the mini-sub made a hissing sound and they felt the grinding of metal. The sub lurched under them.

"That didn't sound right," Cleo said. "Maybe the sub is as new to docking as we are to spy work."

"I'll look at the hatch," Evan said.

He crawled to the back of the mini-sub. The control panel read:

Attachment: READY
Air Lock: READY
Mini-sub Hatch: READY
Docking Hatch: ERROR

"It's blinking red," Cleo said. "Red is bad."

Evan spun the wheel on the hatch. The mini-sub made another hissing noise and the door swung open. He ran his hand along the base's hatch. It was the only thing that stood between them and the inside of the Viper's lair. And it was perfectly smooth.

"Maybe it has to open from the inside," Evan said.

"Should we knock?" Cleo asked.

Evan pushed against the heavy hatch. It wouldn't budge. He pressed the sub's control panel to see if it would unlock the door, but the red light kept blinking.

"Hey, what about your watch?" Cleo suggested.

"Who cares how many footsteps I've taken today?" Evan said.

"No, the laser," Cleo said. "We could cut right through the door."

Evan thought about it. "If we do that, when we need to escape, we won't be able to detach without flooding this evil, skull-shaped secret base."

"Who cares?" Cleo said. "It's an evil, skull-shaped secret base."

"Good point," Evan said. He rolled up his sleeve and pointed his wrist at the base's hatch. He pressed the button. The green laser shot out. The metal sparked and then began to melt.

"It smells like cheese burning inside a toaster oven," Cleo said while Evan worked the laser in a slow circle. Finally, a hunk of metal dropped into the mini-sub. Smoke rose from its edges.

"Let's go," Cleo said. She pushed past Evan and climbed through the hole into the secret base.

Evan climbed in after her.

The hallways were round and lit by bright lights. Evan and Cleo ran as quietly as they could, passing doorways that led in different directions.

"Which way do we go?" Cleo asked.

Evan looked around. "I have no idea," he said.

"Halt!" The voice came from behind them. Two men in green uniforms with gold buttons ran toward them. They wore dark helmets with visors that covered their eyes and leather gloves that were clenched tight.

"Those fists look like they're ready for punching," Cleo said. "Run!"

Evan and Cleo darted down a side hallway. They made a few quick turns and came to a room filled with crates.

"A storage room," Evan said. "What's in those boxes over there?"

Cleo scanned the labels. "Supplies. Towels, toilet paper, bottled water, a few spools of twine." She grabbed the twine and tucked it in her pocket. "Twine is useful."

"For what?" Evan asked.

"All sorts of stuff," Cleo said. "Tying packages, playing string games, fishing, kite flying, anything!"

"Are you planning on flying a kite today?" Evan asked.

"You never know," Cleo said, looking through another crate. "Ewww."

"What?" Evan said.

"Sardines in olive oil. Sardines are gross."

"This crate has a whole bunch of mirrors in it," Evan said. "Let me think."

But there wasn't time. Because just then the door to the storage room slid open.

CHAPTER 5

"We know you're in here," one of the hench-men growled. "It smells like fear."

Evan crouched behind the crate and slid a mirror out of one of the boxes. He leaned it against the wall at the end of an aisle so he could see the whole storage room. Cleo was hiding behind the supply shelf. Evan motioned for her to toss him a few cans of sardines.

"What?" she mouthed silently.

Evan made a fish face and pointed to the shelves.

Cleo nodded.

Evan glanced in the mirror. The henchmen were just coming into view. Something smacked into the back of his head. Sardine cans clattered to the floor.

He glared at Cleo.

"Sorry," she mouthed.

The henchmen spun around. "There you are," one of them said.

Both henchmen ran down the aisle. Evan could see them in the mirror's reflection. He grabbed the tab on the sardine can and twisted as quickly as he could. He risked a glance up. The men were only a few feet away. He dumped the sardines on the floor. The fish spilled out with a slimy, squishy squelch.

One henchman skidded on the slippery fish and fell on his face. The second henchman tripped over him. They both slid into the mirror, which tipped over and smashed into a million pieces.

"Looks like you two are going to have seven years of bad luck," Evan said.

"That line was much better," Cleo said.

Evan leaped over the henchmen. "Go!" he called to Cleo.

They darted out of the room and ran down the hallway, turning and twisting until Evan spotted something useful.

"Wait," Evan said. "There!"

He ran to a control panel on the wall of the hallway and began tapping at the touch screen. "Maybe I can find out where Agent Dearth is being held." He tapped a few icons and pulled up a map of the base. "It looks like he's in a holding cell in the grotto," Evan said.

"What's a grotto?" Cleo asked.

"It's an underwater cave. The base must be connected to it."

"Whoa," Cleo said.

"It's not *that* interesting," Evan said.

"No," Cleo said. "Whoa to that."

Evan turned to look where Cleo was staring. Behind him loomed a giant bubble-shaped window. In the darkness of the water, schools of tiny fish swam by. The fish glowed different colors, creating swirls of pink, blue, and green.

"We must be in one of the eyes of the skull," Cleo said. "Kind of makes you want to have a secret, evil, underwater base all your own."

Evan nodded. "All except the evil part."

He turned back around. "The grotto is down a spiral staircase and along a rocky tunnel." Evan stopped. He heard a footstep. "What was that?" he asked.

"It sounded like a footstep," Cleo said.

Evan rolled his eyes.

A man rounded the corner. He was dressed in green like the other henchmen, but he was much, much bigger. His arms were thicker than pythons. His fists were like wrecking balls. His head was so large that his henchman helmet looked like it might pop off.

"Give up and I will not harm you," the giant said in a deep voice.

"I don't think that's a good idea," Evan said.

"If I have to chase you, I may become upset," the giant said. "You don't want to see me upset."

"Actually," Cleo said, "I don't want to see you at all."

She and Evan turned and ran. They tried

to lose the giant henchman. But he was much quicker than he seemed. His footsteps and his angry grunts were never far behind them.

"There!" Evan said, pointing to a spiral staircase that led downward. "This must be the way to the grotto."

"I have an idea," Cleo said. She pulled the twine from her pocket and tied it to the railing. She strung it through one of the loops on the other side of the staircase and crouched in a small nook.

"What are you doing?" Evan asked.

"Get him to chase you down the stairs," Cleo said.

"Are you crazy?" Evan said. "I'm not going to ask an overgrown bulldozer to come after me."

"Just trust me," Cleo said.

Evan called out to the henchman. "Hey, giant! I've got your golden goose over here!"

"No one calls me a giant except my mom!" the henchman hollered.

He lumbered toward them.

Evan darted past Cleo down the spiral staircase.

Just as the henchman came near, Cleo yanked on the twine. The strand caught the henchman's foot and he fell forward. His head struck the metal railing and he tumbled down the stairs.

Evan ran as fast as he could, but the giant kept falling. Evan leaped to the bottom and ducked to the side just in time to miss getting steamrolled by four hundred pounds of henchman. Cleo came down the stairs to find the giant out cold.

"The bigger they come, the harder they fall," Evan said.

They ran down a rocky tunnel and came to a sliding door.

Evan pressed the button on a nearby control panel. "It's locked," he said.

Cleo fished her magnetic lock pick out of her pocket and held it against the panel. "I didn't think this would come in handy."

"Hurry," Evan said. "That goon is starting to move."

"I'm hurrying as fast as I can," Cleo said.

She pressed the button on her gadget, and the display panel flickered. Sparks flew out of it and it began to smoke. Then, like magic, the door slid open.

"Huh," Cleo said. "It worked."

As they rushed through the doorway, a

voice called out to them. "Out of the frying pan and into the fire."

Steam rose from a wide crater in the center of the room. A single henchman wearing a gold badge stood on a catwalk that circled above them. The henchman stalked along the catwalk to a ladder and climbed down.

"It took you long enough to get here." The henchman's sharp-heeled boots made a familiar clicking sound on the stone floor.

"Ms. Crowley," Evan said.

She took off her helmet and her hair tumbled across her shoulders. Somehow, she looked more glamorous than the kids had ever seen her.

"I followed you into this book," she said, "just like you followed me into *The Case of the Mysterious Moonstone*. I'm playing the role of Katrina Ivanovich, the head henchman."

"You mean hench*woman*," Cleo said.

Ms. Crowley tapped the badge on her chest. "Whatever I am, we're on opposite sides," she said. "If I don't try to stop you, the story will be ruined and none of us will get out of this book."

"But if we stop you . . ." Evan said. "You might end up . . ."

"I may end up stuck in this book forever," Ms. Crowley said, crossing her arms. "Many librarians have been lost in books just like this one. No one is sure what happens when you get stuck, whether you're doomed to play out the story over and over every time someone reads the book or if you're able to continue as the person you've become after the tale ends. What we do know is that time in our world moves very slowly when we're in a story. What feels like days here will only be a few minutes in our world."

"Either way it's scary," Cleo said.

Evan nodded and thought about his parents. How would they feel if he just disappeared one day? Then he thought about Ms. Hilliard. No matter what, they needed to find her. "So, Ms. Hilliard . . ."

Ms. Crowley tensed. "Ms. Hilliard disappeared into one of these books," she said. "I'm her replacement."

"You're nothing like her," Cleo muttered.

"We have to play this story out," Ms. Crowley said. "Fiction works in strange ways, and we have to follow the rules."

"What do you mean?" Cleo asked.

Ms. Crowley cracked her knuckles. "What I mean . . ." Ms. Crowley said, ". . . is this!"

Before Evan and Cleo could even blink, their nasty librarian dove straight at them.

CHAPTER 6

Evan and Cleo leaped out of the way. No matter how mean Ms. Crowley was, neither of them could bring themselves to hit her. Anyhow, she was twice their size.

So, they ran.

They scampered up the ladder to the catwalk. But Ms. Crowley was already chasing after them.

"This spy stuff means a lot of running!" Evan said.

"Good thing I play soccer," Cleo said.

"Trombone is more about sitting," Evan panted.

They wound around the catwalk and turned a corner. They came to an open ledge that dropped thirty feet to the stone floor.

"There isn't anywhere to go," Cleo said. "We're in trouble."

Ms. Crowley rounded the corner behind them. "Nowhere to run," she said.

"You forgot one thing," Evan said. He looked around at the maze of catwalks criss-crossing high above the steaming crater until his eyes fell on the spot where the one they stood on was bolted to the jagged wall.

Ms. Crowley stepped toward them. "What did I forget?" she said.

"We're the main characters in this story,"

he said. "Main characters always find a way to win."

Evan pointed his wrist and pressed the button on his watch. A green laser shot out. The beam struck the metal bolt. Sparks flew into the air. The catwalk groaned and pulled away from the wall. Evan, Cleo, and Ms. Crowley stumbled as it began to fall.

"Jump!" Evan screamed.

Evan and Cleo leaped into open air. They barely made it to another walkway and managed to pull themselves up.

Ms. Crowley wasn't so lucky. She stumbled forward and rolled off the end of the catwalk. She spun as she fell and grabbed on to the railing. Soon she was dangling high above the steaming crater.

"Do me a favor," Ms. Crowley said to them.

"What?" Cleo said.

"Tell . . . my sister . . . I tried . . ."

And with those words, Ms. Crowley's fingers slipped from the metal and she plummeted into the crater. A puff of steam burst from the hole in the ground and she was gone.

"Oh no," Evan said.

Evan and Cleo rushed to the ladder and climbed down to the stone floor.

Evan began pacing nervously. "What do we do?"

"We need to finish this story."

"Our librarian just fell into a volcanic pit!" Evan said.

"I know," Cleo said, "but she was playing her role. Now we have to play ours. We need to defeat the Viper and rescue Agent Dearth."

"Okay," Evan said. He wasn't so sure

anymore, but he liked that Cleo was taking charge. "What do we do now?"

"The map said the grotto is somewhere behind that wall."

Evan looked where Cleo was pointing. "But there's no door," he said.

"We have to find it."

Evan went over to one of the computer monitors. It showed a grid of squares, five across and five down. Different boxes had different letters in them, A through D:

D				B
	A	C		
		D		
C	A	B		

The instructions at the bottom of the screen read: Connect each letter with its match by moving up or down, left or right. Do not cross any of your lines or you'll be in for a nasty surprise! All squares must be used in the solution. Press START to begin.

"It looks like a puzzle," Evan said, "a very dangerous puzzle."

Cleo came over and read the instructions. "Looks easy enough," she said.

She pressed START and the door they had come in slammed shut.

"I'm not sure it's as easy as it looks," Evan said.

"Oh, don't be a baby," she said. She touched the letter D and dragged her finger three boxes down and two to the right. The trail of her finger left a purple line in the boxes she crossed.

"Wait," Evan said. "Now you've trapped the C in the corner."

Cleo touched the C and slid her finger up, but as soon as the new line crossed the purple line, a buzzer sounded and the screen cleared. The floor rumbled and a burst of steam rose from the crater. The room got hotter.

"We need to think about this," Evan said. He touched the letter A in the middle of the grid and slid his finger straight down to the other A. A yellow line connected the boxes.

"Try B now," Cleo suggested.

Evan looked at the two Bs in the grid. There was a lot of free space on that side of the board, but he felt as though there might be a trick.

"Just do this," Cleo said. She reached

across and touched her finger on the B at the bottom of the grid. She slid one to the right, up to the top of the grid, and another to the right. Her finger left a pink trail.

"Ooh, my favorite color," she said.

The screen buzzed and the empty boxes toward the right lower part of the puzzle blinked. More steam burst from the crater. Lava began to bubble out and ooze along the floor.

"Stop messing with my puzzlc," Evan said.

"Well, you can't just stare at it all day!"

"It's better than getting covered in lava!" Evan said.

The screen cleared and Evan took a deep breath. He connected the As.

Evan felt the heat from the lava. He glanced back to see it spreading across the floor toward them.

"Hurry!" Cleo said.

He connected the Bs along the bottom and up the right side.

Cleo inched nearer to Evan as the lava crept closer.

But he concentrated on the grid. The lower D could only connect by going one toward the right, up the right side, and across the top. Evan trailed his finger along the boxes, turning them light blue.

"Come on!" Cleo pleaded. "My boots are sizzling!"

Evan looked at the boxes. There was only one pathway for C. He nervously traced his finger along it.

The screen flashed green and they heard a grinding noise. The wall slid open.

Evan and Cleo rushed through the opening and the door slid shut behind them. They both sighed loudly. Sweat trickled down their faces.

"I take back what I said about puzzles being boring," Cleo said.

This room was much cooler than the lava-filled computer room. It was a dark cave with a calm pool of water in the center. A man in a red suit stood at the water's edge. When he turned, Evan recognized his perfect teeth and slicked-back golden hair.

"Agent Dearth!" Evan called out. "We're Agents Evan and Cleo. We're here to rescue you from the Viper."

"It's you who needs rescuing," the man said as four henchmen filed in behind him. "Super-secret agent Samuel Dearth *is* the Viper!"

CHAPTER 7

In minutes, Evan and Cleo were tied back-to-back and strung upside down over the dark pool in the grotto.

"We seem to have a predicament," the Viper said.

"What's a predicament?" Cleo asked.

"A problem," Evan explained.

"Of course we have a problem," Cleo said. "We're hanging upside down over a pool!"

"Not just any pool," the Viper said. He picked up a bucket of fish and dumped it into the water. The surface began to bubble and thrash. Shiny gray fins broke the surface. "Say hello to my man-eating sharks."

"We don't *need* to have a predicament," Evan said. "You could just lower us down and let us go. We could discuss this over some toast and oleo."

"Ah, you'd like that, wouldn't you?" the Viper said. "Wait, what's oleo?"

"Hah!" Cleo said. "I told you no one uses that word!"

The Viper came closer. "I have big plans, and I don't want the two of you to mess them up. Plus, my little pets do need their lunch."

"Actually, your sharks seem a little chubby,"

Evan said. "Today might be a good time to start a diet."

The Viper pulled a red lever next to the pool of water. A timer on the wall started counting down. "In five minutes, the cable holding you will release, dropping you into the shark pool. Farewell, Agent Evan and Agent Cleo!"

Evan looked down. The sharks circled faster. One leaped out of the water and snapped its jaws.

"Wait!" Cleo said. "Why are you doing all of this? Why did you leave A.C.R.O.N.Y.M. to become an evil mastermind?"

The Viper clasped his hands behind his back and turned to them. "I suppose there's no harm in letting you in on my secrets," he said. "I spent years risking my life for Avery Phillips and A.C.R.O.N.Y.M. What did they ever do for me?"

"They paid you money," Evan said. "That's how jobs work."

"No amount of money is worth risking your life every day. It was always, 'Hey, Agent Dearth, let's parachute you into the jungles of Central America to stop a madman from getting his hands on a deadly poison,' or 'Agent Dearth, let's fire you off in a rocket to sabotage some giant laser satellite.' Not once did Avery Phillips ever think of what I want!"

"What do you want?" Cleo asked.

The Viper's eyebrows pushed together as he thought. "I don't know, but that's not the point! The point is that it's time for me to get something out of the whole spy game."

He picked up a black box from the floor. "This hard drive has the names and secret identities of every spy in A.C.R.O.N.Y.M. as well as all the top secret information ever gathered by the agency. I'm going to sell it to the highest bidder and disappear."

"But that will put hundreds of agents at risk!" Evan said.

"Not hundreds," the Viper said. "Thousands. I have every bit of useful information our enemies want: the locations of secret hideouts and details on all our gadget technology."

"That's evil!" Cleo said.

"Exactly," the Viper said. "Now, if you'll excuse me, I have a date with my escape pod."

The Viper and his henchmen laughed and left the grotto.

"Avery said we wouldn't need harpoon guns on this mission," Cleo said. "A harpoon gun would be pretty useful right now."

"What are we going to do?" Evan asked. "The timer is down to two minutes."

Another shark burst from the surface of the water. This one jumped closer than the last. Evan could smell its fishy breath as it snapped its jaws beneath them.

Cleo wriggled. "If we start to swing, we can time it so that we're not over the shark pool when the cable releases. It's our only chance."

"How do we swing?" Evan asked.

"Squeeze your stomach muscles."

"How do I squeeze my stomach muscles?" Evan said.

"You know, like you're doing sit-ups."

"Sit-ups are not my thing," Evan said.

"Just do it!" Cleo hollered.

Evan bent as though he was trying to lift his chin to his knees. When he released, he and Cleo moved a little. As they swung backward, Cleo bent and they moved a little more.

They took turns that way until they started to swing back and forth. With each swing, they swayed farther and farther from the center of the shark pool.

Evan glanced at the timer. "We're down to thirty seconds," he cried out.

"Swing harder!" Cleo barked.

Evan's stomach burned. "I'm swinging as hard as I can!"

"It's not enough!"

The sharks began thrashing as though they could already taste their next meal.

A computerized voice began to count down from ten. Tears streaked from Evan's eyes as he strained forward and back.

Finally, the timer reached zero. The cable released. Evan leaned forward with all of his strength. They swung clear of the shark pool and landed hard on the stone floor.

"That was close!" Cleo said excitedly.

"My stomach is killing me!" Evan whined. "And we're still tied up!"

A voice came from behind them. "Not for long."

Evan and Cleo twisted around.

"Ms. Crowley!" Evan cried out.

"I am not Ms. Crowley," Ms. Crowley said. "Remember, I am Katrina Ivanovich, and I've got a score to settle with the Viper."

CHAPTER 8

"We thought you were . . ." Evan said. "We thought you fell into the lava crater!"

"Head henchwomen don't die so easily," Ms. Crowley said as she untied them. "Anyhow, I've got to stop the Viper."

"Why?" Cleo asked, getting up and dusting off her wet suit. "I thought you were working *for* the Viper."

"I was, but part of my story is that my sister is an A.C.R.O.N.Y.M. agent. Even though

73

we're on opposite sides, I don't want her to get hurt. Blood is thicker than water. Love conquers all. Blah, blah, blah. Now, let's go."

They raced through the base in search of the Viper.

"How did you get out of the lava crater?" Evan asked as they turned a corner and darted up a flight of metal stairs.

"As I was falling, I grabbed on to a ledge. When I pulled myself up, I found a tunnel that led to the waste disposal room," Ms. Crowley said.

"Waste?" Cleo asked. "That's gross."

"Gross is right," Ms. Crowley said. "Now, follow me. I know where the escape pods are."

The kids followed Ms. Crowley along several hallways, up two more flights of stairs, and through a bunch of high-tech rooms. The escape pod bay was a bright white chamber with six oval hatches nestled in one wall.

The Viper was stepping into one of the hatches. The computer drive was tucked under his arm.

"It's over, Viper," Evan called out.

"Wait," Cleo said. "If he's *the* Viper, should you say, 'It's over, *the* Viper' or is it just 'Viper'?"

"It doesn't really sound right if I say *the* Viper right there," Evan said. "I'm going to stick with Viper."

"No matter what you say, it's not over," the Viper said. "My henchmen have already left in the other escape pods, and I've set the self-destruct timer for the base. In five minutes, the three of you will be shark chum."

"No!!!" Ms. Crowley yelled as she tackled the Viper. The hard drive spun through the

air and clattered to the ground. The Viper and Ms. Crowley struggled on the floor.

"Blast the hard drive with your laser watch!" Cleo yelled.

Evan aimed his wrist at the hard drive and pressed the button. Nothing happened. He looked at his wrist. The face of the watch was cracked.

"It must have broken when we fell in the grotto," Evan said. "Let's get that hard drive!"

They dove across the room. Evan grabbed the black box and smashed it against the floor. It shattered into a thousand pieces.

"It's a good thing hard drives don't bring bad luck the way mirrors do," Cleo said.

Just then, the Viper pushed Ms. Crowley off of him. Her head banged on the ground with a thud.

The Viper surveyed the smashed hard drive. "No matter," he said. "I've got a copy of those files in the mainframe computer. Just before the base explodes, it will upload all the information to my satellites. Face it. You've lost, Agents Evan and Cleo. Now, I must say good-bye. I'd hate to be here when that timer reaches zero."

And with that, the Viper dove into the hatch and slammed his hand on the release button. The door slid shut and the escape pod detached. The Viper's evil laughter still echoed off the walls.

"I'm so sorry," Ms. Crowley said. "I've failed."

"This story isn't over yet," Evan said.

Ms. Crowley rose to her feet and rubbed her head. "How are we going to escape? All the pods are gone."

"We still have our mini-sub," Evan said. "But first, we need to destroy the stolen files before the base links up with the satellite."

"I know where the mainframe is," Ms. Crowley said.

"Then what are we waiting for?" Cleo said.

A computerized female voice came from above. "Time to self-destruct: three minutes."

"How can that voice stay so calm when everything is about to explode?" Evan asked.

They followed Ms. Crowley until they reached a door. Evan pressed the button to open it, but a red light flashed. "Access denied," a voice said.

Cleo pulled out her magnetic lock pick, but Ms. Crowley pushed her aside. "We don't have time for that," she said. She threw herself forward and slammed her heel against the metal next to the doorknob. The door flung open.

"Whoa," Cleo said. "Where'd you learn to do that?"

"Door kicking school," Ms. Crowley said. "Now, where's that hard drive?"

Evan ran into the room, sat at a keyboard, and began pecking at the keys.

"Do you know what you're doing?" Cleo said, looking over his shoulder.

The calm female voice spoke. "Time to self-destruct: two minutes."

The hard drive lit up and a large gray disk behind thick glass started to spin.

"If ten years of video games have taught me anything, it's how to use a computer," Evan said. He squinted at the screen. "I can delete everything—but it's going to take more than two minutes."

"Is that the hard drive?" Ms. Crowley asked, pointing to the spinning disk.

"That's it," Evan said.

Ms. Crowley strode over and slammed her heel into the thick glass. The glass cracked. The hard drive shook, but it kept whirring. She stomped again. Another slender crack appeared in the glass.

"It's no use!" Ms. Crowley said. "It'll take me an hour to stomp through there!"

"We don't have an hour," Cleo said. "Let me try."

"What are you going to do," Ms. Crowley said, "talk at it until it explodes?"

"No," Cleo said calmly. "I'm going to do this . . ."

Cleo pulled the magnetic lock pick from her pocket. She placed it against the cracked glass and pressed the button. The lights in the hard drive flashed red and the disk started to sizzle. Within seconds, the plastic disk melted and was dripping down the inside of the hard drive. Smoke puffed out of the console.

"Strong magnets mess up computer memory," Cleo said.

"How'd you know that?" Evan asked.

"Last year, my mom's credit cards got erased by the magnetic clasp of her purse. I figured this was the same thing, just much stronger."

"Brilliant!" Evan said. He spun in his chair and bolted for the door. "Let's get to the mini-sub!"

The calm female voice spoke. "Time to self-destruct: one minute." Then the voice began counting down each second from sixty.

"Wait!" Cleo called out, pointing to the computer monitor. "Evan, look! Purple, sparkly letters."

"We don't have time to read your girly notes," Ms. Crowley said.

But Evan knew that purple and sparkly were two of Ms. Hilliard's favorite things. It had to be her. He read quickly:

Dear Evan,

I expect you only have a moment to read this, so I'll be brief. First, I know there's little I can do to stop you from continuing on. Please use all caution. Also, understand that sometimes people you think are against you may be your friend after all.

Now, pay attention to that countdown.

That calm computerized voice means business. RUN!

Your friend and librarian,
Ms. Hilliard

"Let's go!" Ms. Crowley hollered from the doorway.

Evan, Cleo, and Ms. Crowley raced down the hallway until Evan spotted the broken hatch door he'd melted open. The sub was still attached.

The computerized voice continued counting down the seconds.

"Thirty-nine . . . Thirty-eight . . ."

"Hurry!" Cleo cried, hopping in first.

Ms. Crowley went next, followed by Evan, who slammed the sub's hatch shut and slapped his hand on the airlock button.

A buzzer sounded. "Airlock jammed," the computer said.

"I am so sick of calm computerized voices bringing us bad news," Evan said. "The base's hatch won't close because we destroyed it. The sub won't release."

"Sit down!" Cleo said. "I'll put the sub in reverse."

She pulled back on the controls and the mini-sub's motor started whirring. Metal groaned. The sub lurched and tilted.

Twenty-nine . . . Twenty-eight . . .

"Give it more power!" Ms. Crowley said. "We're pulling away!"

"Our hatch might tear off!" Cleo said.

"We're attached to a secret underwater base that's about to explode," Evan said. "We don't have much of a choice."

Cleo pulled harder on the controls. Metal groaned louder and the mini-sub tilted more.

"It's working!" Evan said.

Finally, the sub broke free. "Hang on!" Cleo said. She spun the steering wheel and the sub twisted in the water. Then she slammed the controls forward. The sub surged ahead.

Nineteen . . . Eighteen . . . Seventeen . . .

"Hurry!" Evan said. "We need to be far from the base when it explodes."

"I'm giving it everything I can!" Cleo said.

"We're not going fast enough," Ms. Crowley said.

"How far do you think—" But before Evan could finish, an explosion flashed through the windows of the base. One of the skull's eyes collapsed inward and everything began to quake.

Evan rushed to Cleo's side and scanned

the dashboard. Then he found what he was looking for. He slapped his hand down on a small button that looked like a flame.

Blue fire shot out the back of the mini-sub and they rocketed ahead.

The secret underwater base exploded behind them. The force of the blast flipped the mini-sub around and the hull buckled. Bolts popped loose and clattered around. Ms. Crowley screamed as she tumbled.

Cleo twisted the controls and righted the mini-sub.

Then everything went quiet except for the ping of the sonar.

"Ahoy, ahoy," a voice said. A monitor flickered to life. It was Avery Phillips. "Agent Evan, Agent Cleo, are you okay?"

Evan pressed the communicator button. "We're fine," he said. "Just a little shaken up."

"Yeah," Cleo added, "like a can of whipped cream."

"Now that our signal can reach you, we've activated autopilot," Avery said. "You'll be back to base in a few hours."

"Big roger and big wilco," Evan said.

Cleo leaned back. Evan leaned back. Even Ms. Crowley leaned back. They were exhausted. Within a few moments all three of them were asleep.

CHAPTER 9

By the time they arrived at A.C.R.O.N.Y.M. headquarters, Evan was so sore, he could hardly move. Even a month of playing trombone wouldn't hurt this badly. Cleo looked just as worn out.

"Ah, I see you've captured the nasty Katrina Ivanovich," Avery said.

Several agents grabbed Ms. Crowley and held her by the shoulders.

"The Viper and I would have gotten away with our plot if it weren't for these two!" Ms. Crowley snarled and lunged at Evan and Cleo.

The agents held her back.

"She really takes her role in these books seriously," Cleo whispered.

"I'm not so sure it's an act," Evan said. "She never liked us in the first place."

"Where is Agent Dearth?" Avery asked.

"I hate to bring bad news," Evan said, "but Agent Dearth *is* the Viper."

"That . . . that can't be true," Avery said.

"I'm afraid it is," Cleo said.

"And it's a good thing A.C.R.O.N.Y.M. was here to stop him," Evan said.

"Yeah," Cleo added. "Every time the Viper sticks his head up, we'll be there to smack it down."

"Like a giant game of Smack-a-Mole!" Evan said.

Everyone looked at Evan.

"Was that a little much?" he asked.

Cleo nodded.

They went on to explain what they had discovered about the Viper's plot and how they, with the help of Katrina Ivanovich, had foiled him.

Avery looked at Ms. Crowley. "So, you . . . helped them?"

"I have my reasons," Ms. Crowley said.

"I'm looking forward to getting this wet suit off, taking a nice bath, and sleeping for a few days," Evan said.

"I wish I could tell you to do just that," Avery said, "but we have a new crisis."

"A new crisis?!?!" Evan and Cleo said at once.

"Evil mastermind Baron von Schlecht has tunneled into the deepest vaults of the Bank of Switzerland and has stolen six tons of gold," Avery explained. "We'll bring you to the Alps by chopper and drop you on a mountaintop. You'll evade his guards and ski to the bottom, where you'll find a high-tech sports car parked behind a chalet. You'll drive the car, find Schlecht, and stop him."

"We're on it," Cleo said. "We'll suit up now, get some gadgets from Dr. Omega, and head out tonight."

Evan couldn't believe Cleo was jumping into another adventure. They had barely finished this one, hadn't gotten any closer to finding Ms. Hilliard, and were more exhausted than they'd ever been.

"What are you doing?" Evan said.

"Watch," Cleo answered confidently.

They turned to leave, but as they did, Avery called to them. "Agent Evan, Agent Cleo, you'll need this."

He tossed a key ring to them. Evan and Cleo leaped forward just as Ms. Crowley twisted free of the guards. Together, they jumped up and grabbed the key.

Letters burst from the key like a thousand crazy spiders. The letters tumbled in the air around them and began to spell words. The words became sentences, the sentences paragraphs. Before long, they could barely see through the letter confetti, and then everything went black.

CHAPTER 10

The Lost Library was warm, welcoming, and quiet. Evan was sitting in one of the leather chairs near the crackling fireplace. Cleo sat across from him. She was holding the key to the high-tech sports car. Both of them were back in their school clothes.

"That was crazy," Evan said. He felt like this was the first time he could exhale in a long while.

"I thought it was kind of fun," Cleo said. "I wonder what book this key will unlock."

"We don't have time to find out," Evan said. "We need to get back to class."

"Exactly!" Ms. Crowley said. She stood on a balcony above them. "You need to get to class. But first, give me that key."

Cleo sprang to her feet and started toward the door. "I didn't quite hear you, Ms. Crowley."

Ms. Crowley made her way to a brass ladder and climbed down. "I said, give me that key. It's not safe in your slippery little hands. Anyhow, I need it for my own reasons."

Evan looked up at Ms. Crowley. "In the book, you said something about having a sister . . ."

"Nonsense," Ms. Crowley scoffed. "That was all part of the story—just something to

help me switch sides so we could all get out of the book together."

Evan and Cleo moved toward the stairs that led up to their school library. "We've really got to be getting to class," Evan said. "I think I heard the bell ring."

"No, you didn't," Ms. Crowley said angrily. "It's still recess."

"Great," Evan said. "We'll join our classmates outside today."

"I still have you both for two hundred and fifty-six detentions," Ms. Crowley said.

Evan's heart began to pound. He had never had detention before, and now he was probably setting some sort of record.

"I don't think so," Cleo said. "We'll bring the key back when we're ready. If you're around, maybe you can join us. You made a good sidekick today."

Ms. Crowley scowled. "Tomorrow," she said.

Evan and Cleo took the stairs two at a time, weaved their way out of the library, and burst out of the double doors onto the playground.

Cleo tossed the key into the air, caught it, and stuffed it into her pocket. "Looks like we've got plans for recess tomorrow, Agent Evan."

"Roger and wilco, Agent Cleo," Evan said. "Roger and wilco."

The Lost Library is full of exciting—and dangerous—books! And Evan and Cleo have a magical key to open one of them. Where will they end up next? Read on for a sneak peek of *The Haunted Howl*!

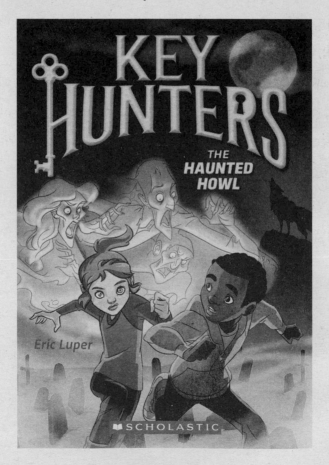

CHAPTER 1

"Have you seen Ms. Crowley today?" Evan asked Cleo across the library table.

"No," Cleo said. "It's weird because she's usually hanging around with her clicky high heels and her screechy voice."

They were already halfway through recess, and Evan and Cleo had a job to do. They needed to get another step closer to finding their former librarian, Ms. Hilliard, who mysteriously disappeared into one of the magical books in the secret library beneath their school.

"What are you working on?" Cleo asked.

Evan pushed away his book. "A gross report."

"What's gross about it?"

"It's about bats," Evan said. "Few things scare me more than bats."

"Have you ever seen a live bat up close?"

"I don't need to see one up close to know they're gross."

Cleo looked at the book. "They're kind of cute, like dwarf hamsters. I'd call this one Moe and that one Sprinkles."

"I'd call *you* crazy."

"I'd call me bored," Cleo said. "Let's go."

Evan and Cleo found their way to the farthest shelf in the darkest corner of the library—to the shelf that hid the secret door that led to the magical library. Cleo laced her fingers and boosted Evan up until he was eye level with a huge, dusty, boring-looking book titled *Literature: Elements and Genre from Antiquity to Modern-Day*.

Before Evan could pull out the book, Cleo groaned and lowered him back to the floor.

"What's the matter?" Evan asked.

"My shoulders are sore from Ansley Teal's birthday party last night."

"Your shoulders are sore from a birthday party?" Evan asked.

"The party was at Adventure Time Rock Gym. Rock climbing is really hard. We learned all about rappelling and harnesses and carabiners."

Evan pretended to know what she was talking about. He rolled a stool over, carefully climbed up, and pulled on the book. It tipped forward and the secret bookcase swung open. The stairway that led to the hidden room under their school library was darker than usual.

"Don't you think it's weird that Ms. Crowley isn't around?" Evan asked as they went down.

"Maybe she's on break or something," Cleo said.

The magical library was darker than Evan remembered. Shelves, sliding ladders, and spiral staircases stretched into the darkness above them. Catwalks and balconies reached around corners and across gaps to let readers explore every nook. At the back of the library, over a stone fireplace, hung a tapestry that showed an open book with people swirling into it among a sea of colorful letters. The fireplace was already lit, but dimmer than usual.

"Does the library look creepy today?" Evan asked.

Cleo shrugged. "It always looks creepy to me."

They crept along the library wall. Evan pulled out the key they had gotten on their last adventure. It was the key to a fancy sports car given to them by the head of a secret spy organization.

"Which book do you think it unlocks?" Evan asked.

"I don't know. Why don't we ask the woman in that painting?"

They looked at the painting that hung just above them. Evan didn't remember ever seeing it hanging there before. It showed a woman wearing a yellow dress and a crown.

Her eyes seemed to follow them wherever they moved.

Suddenly, the canvas of the painting began to stretch out toward them. The woman's hands reached out from of the painting and swiped at them.

Cleo let out a scream. Then she and Evan ran.

They climbed a ladder and darted across a catwalk. But when they hurried around a corner, they bumped straight into their current librarian, Ms. Crowley.

"I've been waiting to grab that key from you!" she said. She reached for Cleo, but Cleo ducked.

The kids slid down a brass pole, and that's when they spotted it. A locked book lay closed on the table in the center of the room. The cover was made of cracked leather and covered in dust. The title read *The Werewolf's Curse.*

"Give me the key," Cleo said.

"I am *not* going into a werewolf story," Evan said.

"You want to rescue Ms. Hilliard, right?"

Ms. Crowley was already sliding down the pole, her sharp, clicky heels scraping against the metal. "Come here!" she screeched. "I need that key!"

Evan shifted from one foot to the other. He had told Cleo that few things scared him more than bats. Werewolves were one of those things.

But then he thought about Ms. Hilliard. She needed their help.

Evan handed her the key.

"Don't go without me!" Ms. Crowley cried.

Cleo jammed the key into the lock and turned it. The lock popped open. Letters burst from the pages of the book like a thousand crazy spiders. They tumbled in the air around them and began to spell words. The words turned into sentences, the sentences paragraphs. Before long, they could barely see through the letter confetti.

Then everything went black.

CHAPTER 2

Pain burned deep in Evan's arm. Sweat trick-led down his forehead. He opened his eyes. He was lying on a bed in a dim shack. Cleo and a boy Evan didn't recognize stood over him. Cleo's hair was pulled back. She was wearing a plain gray dress with a white apron. The boy's skin was pale and looked paper-thin.

"Who... are you?" Evan asked.

"The fever has clouded his mind," the boy said. "We must act quickly."

Cleo touched Evan's cheek. "What fever?"

"He has been bitten."

"Bitten?" Evan said. "Like by a mosquito?"

The boy looked stern. "Evan, you've been bitten by a werewolf."

"How do you know my name?" Evan asked.

The boy looked worried. "It's me, Francis, son of the village doctor. You're Evan, the baker's son, and this is Cleo, the blacksmith's daughter. We've been friends since we were tots."

Evan thought the word 'tot' sounded funny. He chuckled and began to sit up, but dizziness overcame him and he lay back down.

"If I hadn't pulled you into my family's home, the mob would have gotten you," Francis said.

"What mob?"

"The *angry* mob, of course," Francis said. "Tonight is the full moon. At midnight, you'll undergo your first transformation. It won't be easy."

Evan shook his head. "I really don't think—"

Francis grabbed Evan's arm and rolled up the sleeve. A burning line of red dots circled his forearm near his elbow.

"You were bitten," Francis said. "Some say getting *eaten* by a werewolf is better than being *bitten* by one."

Cleo peeked out the curtains. "It's already getting dark," she said. "Should we tie Evan to the bed and stay with him until morning?"

"I'm afraid that won't work," Francis said. "When he transforms, the bed will break into splinters and the rope torn to bits… along with us."

"Seriously, guys," Evan said, sitting up. "I'm feeling better…"

Evan stopped. He sniffed at the air. He could smell the oil from the dim lamp, the earthy wool of the blanket, the stale hay inside the mattress, all in more detail than he could ever remember noticing.

"Weird," Evan whispered.

Evan sniffed again. The hairs on his neck stood up. He smelled swampy mud and nervous sweat. He heard shallow breathing. There was someone behind the door.

Evan sprang from the bed. He surprised himself by how far he was able to leap. He landed softly, took two steps, and flung open the door. A hunched figure disappeared around the corner of the building.

"We can't stay here," Francis said. He loaded a small jar, some papers, a coil of rope, and a few other supplies into a leather bag and slung it over his shoulder.

"What do we do?" Evan asked.

"There is a way to get rid of the werewolf inside you," Francis said.

"Call animal control?" Cleo asked.

"No. A cure," Francis said. "We need to find leaves of wolfsbane, sprinkle it into water collected from a flowing stream, and stir it with the silver Lycan Spoon under the light of a full moon."

"I'm turning into a werewolf in a few hours and you want to throw a tea party?" Evan said.

"It's more like a potion."

"How do you know all this stuff?" Cleo asked.

"My father studied it for years. Everyone said he was crazy—that it was too dangerous—but he wanted to end this curse once and for all."

"Where's your father now?"" Evan asked.

A tear rolled down Francis's cheek. "You already know this," Francis said. "My father disappeared several months ago. He left the village to confront the werewolves with his cure. He hasn't been back since."

"I'm guessing there aren't any wolfsbane shops in this village," Cleo said.

Francis reached past her and flung open the curtains.

"We'll find it there," he said, pointing into the darkness.

A flash of lightning lit the night. An old mansion sat atop a rocky mountain. A single, jagged path led up to it through a dark forest.

"We must gather the wolfsbane in the haunted cemetery," Francis said. "Then, we climb the path. It is said there is a waterfall there where we can collect our water. Finally, we'll find the spoon inside the mansion's crumbling walls."

"Why can't we use any old spoon?" Evan asked. "That house looks creepy."

"The Lycan Spoon has special powers. It was crafted from the leg bone of the first werewolf."

"Uh… gross," Cleo said.

"It's the only thing that will save Evan," Francis said. "The road to the old mansion is dangerous. But the mansion itself contains horrors that would make the bravest man weep."

"So why are you helping us?" Evan asked.

"I need to finish my father's work," Francis

said. "It's the only way to save the village. Plus, we've been friends since we were tots."

"You're going to have to stop saying 'tots'," Evan said.

Something howled in the distance. The sound echoed around them, then disappeared in the night. Then came another howl, this one closer.

"Grab your cloaks," Francis said. "We must be quick."

CHAPTER 3

The moon peeked from behind the clouds, lighting the streets of the village. Francis led Evan and Cleo along a narrow alleyway until they came to a stack of firewood. They crouched down behind it.

"That mansion is an evil place!" a man called out. He had a round belly and spit flew out of his mouth with each word. He stood on a platform facing a group of townspeople who held torches and pitchforks. "Now Evan, the baker's son, has been bitten. He can't be allowed to remain. It isn't safe for anyone. We need to end this once and for all!"

The crowd roared angrily.

"It's Old Man Jameson," Francis whispered. "He thinks he runs this village. Even though we're so close to a cure, he thinks killing the werewolves is the only solution."

"Sounds like he's a few sandwiches short of a picnic," Cleo said.

Evan sniffed the air. Old Man Jameson stank like rotten eggs and feet. "He's also short a few bars of soap."

"What's a picnic or soap got to do with any of this?" Francis said.

A low growl came from the back of Evan's throat.

"What was that?" Cleo said.

"The transformation has begun," Francis explained. "We must hurry."

As they turned to go, Cleo bumped the firewood. A single log tumbled down. Then another. Suddenly, the whole pile collapsed.

Everyone in the town square turned to look.

"Run," Francis said.

"The baker's son!" Old Man Jameson screamed. "GET THEM!"

The kids bolted. They ran down a side street, then made a few quick turns as Francis led them along a twisted alley. He pointed at a large crate and put his finger over his mouth to quiet them. They ducked behind it just in time.

Seconds later, the mob thundered past as the townsfolk searched for Evan. Angry voices echoed through the night. Evan shrank deeper into the shadows until the glow of their torches faded.

"You can't hide from us forever!" Old Man Jameson called from the distance. "We need to end this curse once and for all!"

"We *will* end it," Francis muttered, "but not with pitchforks and torches."

"Actually, pitchforks and torches sound better than brewing tea," Evan said.

"Never underestimate the power of a good cup of tea. Now, follow me. I know a secret way out of the village."

Francis led them down another alley. They climbed a wall and squeezed between the posts of an old fence. Finally they came to a bridge that crossed a deep gully. On the far side, the branches of the forest were so low and thick they blocked the path. The night was silent as though the crickets were holding their breath.

"Once we begin, there will be no turning back," Francis said.

"What choice do we have?" Cleo said.

"We could wait until midnight and let me snack on those villagers back there," Evan said. "They seem kind of mean."

"They're frightened and upset," Francis said. "Most of them have lost friends or family to the jaws of a werewolf."

Cleo's eyes narrowed. "Then our mission is clear."

As they approached the path, the thick branches parted like giant, bony hands. And just as soon as they crossed into the forest, the branches fell back into place, sealing them inside.

"I guess you were right," Evan said to Francis.

"About what?"

Evan tried to see the bridge or the lights from the village behind them. There was only darkness. "There really is no turning back."

JOIN THE RACE!

It's an incredible adventure through the animal kingdom, as kids zip-line, kayak, and scuba dive their way to the finish line! Packed with cool facts about amazing creatures, dangerous habitats, and more!

SCHOLASTIC

scholastic.com

MEET RANGER

A time–traveling golden retriever with search-and-rescue training . . . and a nose for danger!

KEY HUNTERS

THE MYSTERIOUS MOONSTONE

by Eric Luper

Illustrated by Lisa K. Weber

SCHOLASTIC INC.

For Linda Pratt, and her most excellent okie-dokies and Jenne Abramowitz, who gave me a shot at writing some fun books

No part of this publication may be reproduced, stored in a retrieval system, or transmitted in any form or by any means, electronic, mechanical, photocopying, recording, or otherwise, without written permission of the publisher. For information regarding permission, write to Scholastic Inc., Attention: Permissions Department, 557 Broadway, New York, NY 10012.

Library of Congress Cataloging-in-Publication Data is available.

ISBN 978-1-338-03686-2

12 11 10 9 8 7 6 5 4 3 2 1   16 17 18 19 20 21

Printed in the U.S.A.   40

This edition first printing, September 2016

Book design by Mary Claire Cruz

CHAPTER 1

"There she goes again," Cleo whispered.

Evan closed his joke book. "There who goes again?" he asked.

"Ms. Crowley," Cleo said. "Every day, she disappears into the back of the library."

Not one kid in school liked the new librarian. After Ms. Hilliard left mysteriously at the end of last year, Ms. Crowley swooped in to take the job. Although they both had the same brown eyes, Ms. Hilliard's were warm

and welcoming while Ms. Crowley's were dark and piercing.

Ms. Hilliard also had a sparkly purple book cart. She taught Evan how to find any fact in a moment and helped Cleo find books she liked. Ms. Crowley only made them sit in their seats and stay quiet.

"She's probably shelving books," Evan said. "Librarians love shelving books. Hey, do you know why an elephant uses his trunk as a bookmark?"

"I don't care," Cleo said, peering down the aisle where Ms. Crowley had vanished.

"So he always *nose* where he stopped reading," Evan said. "Get it? An elephant trunk? *Nose?*"

Cleo ignored him and tightened her ponytail. "I'm going to find out what she's up to."

"Bad idea," Evan said, tucking his joke book into his backpack. "Why do you lose recess every day?"

"Because I don't stay in my seat," Cleo said. "But I had a good reason today."

"I'm sure," Evan said.

"Ellie Fishbein took my pencil. I had to get a new one from the pencil cup."

"You didn't have one in your desk?" Evan asked.

"The pencils in the pencil cup are sharper."

"Uh-huh."

"And they fit better in my hand."

"Uh-huh."

"And they have softer erasers." Cleo looked over her shoulder. "I'm going," she said.

"You're *going* to get punished," Evan said. "A *lifetime* without recess."

"Ms. Crowley will be the one who gets punished," Cleo said. "A teacher should never leave two kids alone. We could get hurt."

With that, Cleo darted between the shelves.

Evan knew following her would only lead to trouble, but he didn't want Cleo to think he was chicken. They twisted through the maze of shelves. Every book he'd ever read smiled out at him like a friend. Here, in the library, he had tons of friends.

"Drat!" a voice said. "Which book is it?"

It came from the next aisle. Ms. Crowley was tugging at books and shoving them back into place. "Literature no longer used," she muttered. "What sort of clue is that? All literature is used!"

"Ms. Crowley," Cleo said. "Is everything okay?"

Ms. Crowley spun to face them. An old-looking brass key hung around her neck. "What do you want?"

"We heard a noise back here," Evan said.

"And I suppose you've come to investigate like two little super-sleuths," Ms. Crowley said.

"We thought you might be in trouble," Cleo said.

"Trouble?" Ms. Crowley stood her full height and towered over the kids. Her black shoes had the pointiest toes and the highest heels Evan had ever seen. "What sort of trouble might one find in a school library?"

"A paper cut?" Evan said.

"Go back to your seats," Ms. Crowley said.

"But we were just—" Cleo began.

"You were *just* going back to your seats," Ms. Crowley said. "Not another word from my junior Frank Hardy and Nancy Drew."

Cleo and Evan headed back to their table.

"Awesome," Cleo whispered. "She called me Nancy Drew."

"So what?" Evan said. "I read one of those books once. Nancy Drew sipped tea and ate something called fancy cakes."

"That's the *old* Nancy Drew," Cleo said. "The new Nancy Drew has a hybrid car and a cell phone. Plus, she solves mysteries!"

Suddenly, Ms. Crowley cried out and the kids heard a sliding sound. Cleo and Evan ran back to look, but Ms. Crowley was gone.

CHAPTER 2

"I told you there's something weird going on," Cleo said. She began tugging at the books. "Help me look."

"Ms. Crowley said, 'Literature no longer used,'" Evan said.

"Every second you waste *thinking about* something is a second you miss *doing* something," Cleo said.

Then Evan remembered.

He charged to the front of the library.

A poster hung on the wall behind the desk. The heading read: "Your Friend Dewey." On the left side stood a cartoon kid with big glasses. Down the right side was a list of different Dewey decimal numbers.

He knew the Dewey decimal system was the way libraries organized their books. Librarians were careful that every book got numbered and shelved properly.

Evan had seen the poster plenty of times before. Near the bottom was a section called *Literature*. Evan read that section closely until he found it:

804—LITERATURE: CODE NO LONGER USED
Literature no longer used.

"Follow me!" Evan said.

He led Cleo to the last aisle of the library.

On the top shelf sat an old, leather-bound book. The number *804* was printed on the book's spine. The title read *Literature: Elements and Genre from Antiquity to Modern-Day.*

"That book looks so boring," Cleo said. "What does 'antiquity' even mean?"

"It means the olden days," he said.

"Modern-day to the guy who wrote that book is probably antiquity to us," Cleo said.

"Just help me," he said.

Cleo laced her fingers and boosted Evan up. Evan grabbed the highest shelf he could. His fingers barely reached the top edge of the book. He curled his fingers around it and pulled.

The heavy book tipped forward. Evan thought it was going to crush them. He leaped

out of the way and they tumbled to the ground.

"What did you do that for?" Cleo said, rubbing her shin through her pink tie-dye soccer sock.

Evan didn't answer. He was too busy staring. Where a wall of dusty shelves used to be, a secret door slid open.

CHAPTER 3

Evan looked down a dimly lit stairway. "We should get the custodian," he said.

"We've wasted enough time," Cleo said. "Ms. Crowley needs our help."

Cleo and Evan stepped onto the first stone stair. Their footsteps echoed. The air felt cold. Suddenly, a sliding noise came from behind them.

"The door!" Evan cried out.

But it was too late. The bookcase slid shut.

"What should we do?" Evan said. He searched for a lever that might reopen the door.

"I guess we take the stairs," Cleo said.

"Are you nuts?" Evan said. "There could be trolls down there. Or evil clowns with vampire fangs."

"Don't be silly," Cleo said, starting down the steps.

As they neared the bottom, a warm light glowed ahead of them. They stepped into the room and Evan sucked in a tiny breath.

The school library forty-two steps above them (Evan had counted) was nothing compared to this one. Bigger than a gymnasium, this library was packed with books of all sizes and colors. Wooden shelves trimmed in brass stretched from floor to ceiling. Balconies, rolling ladders, and spiral staircases allowed readers to reach any book they wanted.

At the back of the library, over a stone fireplace, hung a tapestry that showed an image of an open book. Several people swirled out of the book in a sea of colorful letters.

"The fire's lit," Evan said, grabbing Cleo's wrist. "Ms. Crowley couldn't have built a fire this quickly."

"Maybe someone else is here," Cleo said. "Let's look around."

"Hiding would be smarter," Evan said.

Cleo ignored him.

As they walked, Evan stared at all the books. He saw ghost stories, fantasies, sports stories, tales of adventure, and more. He wanted to open one of the books to see what was inside, but each had a lock on the edge like a fancy diary.

"Look," Cleo said. A brown book with a red ribbon between the pages sat on a table.

The key that had been around Ms. Crowley's neck was sticking out of the open lock. The title was printed across the cover:

THE CASE OF THE MYSTERIOUS MOONSTONE

"What is it?" Evan asked.

"It's a book," Cleo said.

Evan rolled his eyes. "I know that. But of all the books in the library, why is this one out?"

"If Ms. Crowley was around, she'd be able to tell us," Cleo said.

"If Ms. Crowley was around, she'd tell us to go back to our seats," Evan said.

Cleo looked past Evan. "Hey, what's that?"

Against the wall lay a book cart. It was turned on its side. One of the shelves was dented and a leg was bent. The cart was sparkly and purple.

"Ms. Hilliard is here!" Cleo said.

"This cart doesn't mean Ms. Hilliard's here," Evan said.

An envelope was tucked between the bars of the book cart. Cleo took the envelope and opened it. The words were printed in purple ink. Cleo read it aloud.

Librarians speak in hushed voices of a magical library that sweeps readers off to different worlds. I never imagined the legends were true—or that one would be right here beneath my school.

If you have found this note, I am trapped somewhere between the covers of these enchanted books.

To find me, travel through these stories and help give each one the ending it deserves. Fail and you will meet the same fate as me.

Succeed and you will discover wonders beyond your dreams. Always look for the **key** that will move you forward on your journey. I've left clues along the way. Just look for my favorite color!

Signed,

Ms. Sandie Hilliard, librarian

P.S. If this is Evan, go get help. The perils are too great, the challenges are too risky. And you are too fragile.

"I'm not fragile," Evan said.

Cleo held back her laughter. "You kinda are," she said. "But do you think Ms. Hilliard is really trapped inside one of these books?"

Evan righted Ms. Hilliard's book cart. It wobbled on its bent leg. "Maybe *The Case of the Mysterious Moonstone* has some answers."

"I don't see how a book can offer us answers," Cleo said.

"Do you realize what you just said?" Evan asked.

Cleo shrugged. "I look up everything on the Internet."

"Are you ready to open the book?" Evan said.

"What kind of question is that?" Cleo said. "It's just a book."

She reached across the table and opened *The Case of the Mysterious Moonstone*. Letters burst from the pages of the book like a thousand crazy spiders. They tumbled in the air around them and began to spell words. The words became sentences, the sentences paragraphs. Before long, they could barely see, and then everything went black.

CHAPTER 4

Evan and Cleo found themselves in a cluttered office. Gas lamps flickered. A large map of London hung over a desk piled high with papers. In the corner, a small bulldog lay curled on a leather chair.

The dog lifted its head and gave a lazy woof.

"Did we . . . ?" Evan began.

"Did we just get sucked into a book?" Cleo said.

"Awesome," Evan whispered. "Do you think Ms. Hilliard—"

Cleo laughed. "What are you wearing?"

Evan had on a dark jacket with buttons down the front and heavy gray pants. He reached up to feel a round felt hat on his head.

"You look worse," Evan said.

Cleo wore a frilly blue dress, which swayed like a bell every time she moved. She blushed. "Don't you dare tell anyone about this," she hissed.

"Judging from the gas lamps and our clothes, we must be in the nineteenth century," Evan said.

"No way," Cleo said. "My grandma was born in the 1950s, and she had electricity. Lightbulbs, television, and everything."

"No, nineteenth century means the eighteen

hundreds," Evan explained. "You have to subtract a century."

"That makes no sense," Cleo said. She started to go on, but a door opened and a young man rushed in.

"Ah, I see you've met Watson," the man said. He wore a long plaid coat, and his hair was messy. He dumped more papers on the desk. Some fluttered to the floor.

"You must be my new assistants. I had no idea you'd be so"—he looked at them—"so young."

"We're not young," Cleo said.

"And a member of the fairer sex, too!" the man said to Cleo.

Cleo shrugged. "I guess I'm fair. One time, I refereed a soccer game and called a penalty on my best friend."

Evan tugged Cleo's sleeve. "I think he means prettier . . . and more fragile."

"I'm not fragile," Cleo said. "If anyone here is 'fairer,' it's Evan."

"I'm Evan," Evan said. "This is Cleo."

"Pleasure to meet you both," the man said, sorting through a messy pile. "My name is Artie Baker. I'm a detective with the London police. You've been sent to help me solve a crime."

"Are you any good?" Cleo asked.

Artie pulled a treat from his pocket and tossed it to Watson. The dog gobbled it down. "Well, I've had a bit of a bad run," Artie said.

"What does that mean?" Cleo said.

"It means I haven't solved a crime lately," Artie said.

"Lately?" Evan asked.

"To be honest," Artie said, ". . . ever."

Cleo and Evan glanced at each other in concern.

"Well, there was *one* case," Artie said. "My mother misplaced the biscuits she'd purchased at the bakery."

"Let me guess," Cleo said. "You ate them."

Artie grinned. "I see I have two fine assistants."

"You look young to be a detective," Cleo said.

Artie leaned in close. "I lied on my application," he whispered. "I'm only sixteen."

"I don't like the sound of this," Cleo muttered.

"So, where do we start?" Evan asked.

"At the beginning," Artie said. "Detectives must gather clues to uncover the truth. We need to find the Musgrave Moonstone."

"Don't you mean the *mysterious* moon-stone?" Cleo asked.

"Whoever called it that?" Artie said.

"That's the title of this book," Cleo said.

"What book?" Artie said.

"She means the Musgrave Moonstone is very mysterious," Evan said.

"What's mysterious, old chap, is that the Musgrave Moonstone has been stolen!" Artie said. "The suspects are at Colonel Musgrave's home. His daughter is to be married tomorrow. The house will soon be filled with people, so we must be swift if we are to solve this mystery."

CHAPTER 5

Evan, Cleo, and Artie heaved open the iron gate and followed the path to the front door. The house loomed above them. Tall windows spanned the gray stone building, and gargoyles stuck out at odd angles. Artie lifted the door knocker and let it fall with a heavy *thunk*.

"Doesn't the moon look strange tonight?" Cleo said. "It's coppery red."

"It's called a blood moon," Artie said. "The morning paper said it only happens

once in a long while. This one began at eight o'clock this evening and will end at midnight exactly."

"Blood moon? Midnight?" Cleo said. "That's creepy."

Evan shuddered. "Not as creepy as this house. Even ghosts would be scared of this place."

"I want you to keep all four eyes open and all four ears sharp," Artie said.

Watson woofed.

"Don't forget about Watson," Cleo said. "Dogs are people, too."

"All right," Artie said. "Six eyes and six ears. Keep them all open. A great deal depends on it."

"What do you mean?" Evan asked.

Artie sighed. "The police chief told me that if I don't solve this crime, I'll be sacked."

"Sacked?" Cleo said.

"Fired," Evan said. "It really *has* been a bad run, huh?"

Artie handed Evan a small leather journal. "I'd like you to keep notes," he said. "Write down anything we uncover. No detail is too small."

Artie raised his hand to the knocker again, but the door swung open before he could grab it.

A tall man wearing an orange turban looked down his nose at them. His white jacket was spotless except for tiny splatters of red on both sleeves. "Hmmm—yes, what can I do for you?"

"My name is Detective Artie Baker. This is Cleo and Evan. We are with the City of London police."

"I am Kumar, the Musgraves' butler," the man said. "Please follow me."

The entryway was huge. A giant crystal chandelier hung down, and rows of swords were mounted on the walls. Stone staircases swept up both sides of the room and met on a second-floor landing where a big grandfather clock sat and smaller chandeliers hung.

"The butler did it," Cleo whispered as they walked down a long hallway. "I've seen a lot of detective shows. The butler always does it."

Artie leaned over and shielded his mouth with his hand. "Falsely accusing someone can get you in trouble," he said. "We need to search for two things: motive and opportunity."

"Motive means finding a reason someone would *want* the Musgrave Moonstone," Evan said.

"It's probably worth a bajillion dollars," Cleo said. "That's reason enough."

"Opportunity means we need to find someone who had a *chance* to steal it," Artie said.

Cleo turned to Kumar. "Excuse me, but how long have you worked for Colonel Musgrave?" she asked.

The butler raised an eyebrow. "I used to be first mate on one of Colonel Musgrave's trade ships," Kumar said. "We were hit by a monsoon and lost our cargo, along with most of the crew. I spent three weeks floating on a crate of tea, fighting off sharks with a broken oar. When I finally saw the colonel again, I returned his crate to him. He offered me my job back, but I no longer had any interest in sailing. The good colonel and I have been together many years, and we trust each other.

I have no family, and when he offered me a job in his home, I took it."

Kumar walked on. He led them to a large room. Any part of the wall that wasn't covered with exotic animal heads was covered with oil paintings of old people. A man with the bushiest mustache Evan had ever seen sat at a desk. He wore a military uniform with gold buttons down the front. A woman paced behind him. Her dress was so poofy she could hide a few beach balls under there.

"Colonel and Lady Musgrave," Kumar announced. "Detective Baker and his companions are here."

"Thank you, Kumar," Colonel Musgrave said.

When Kumar had disappeared, Colonel Musgrave stood. He had a wooden leg on his

left side. "It's a pleasure to meet you," he said. "This is my wife, Agatha."

Lady Musgrave extended her hand and Artie kissed her glove. Watson sniffed at the hem of her dress.

"The police have already searched the house," Colonel Musgrave said. "The moonstone is long gone."

"Don't give up hope," Cleo said.

"You don't understand," Lady Musgrave said. "The Musgrave Moonstone is cursed!"

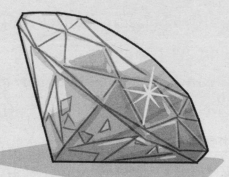

CHAPTER 6

"Cursed?!?" Evan and Cleo said at once.

"Ever since we've had it, the moonstone has brought nothing but trouble!" Lady Musgrave said.

"What sort of trouble?" Artie asked.

The colonel tapped his wooden leg. "In the span of three years, I lost my leg to a Bengal tiger and a dozen ships to pirates. Now, my daughter has fallen ill on the eve of her wedding. I suppose it's best the stone is gone."

Evan scribbled in the journal.

"We're sorry for your losses," Artie said. "Can you tell us about the moonstone?"

Musgrave nodded. "For starters, it's actually a diamond."

"I thought moonstones were opals," Artie said.

Watson woofed in agreement.

"This diamond is called a moonstone because it changes depending on the phase of the moon," Lady Musgrave said.

"How does it do that?" Cleo asked.

"It's a mystery," Colonel Musgrave said. "When the moon is full, the diamond glows a brilliant white. When the moon is dark, it turns gray, almost black. I got it as payment for a large shipment of silk. It's as large as a baby's fist and flawless. Queen Victoria planned to have the stone put on a

crown. It would have made her other jewels seem tiny."

"But when the queen saw the diamond change color, she no longer wanted it," Lady Musgrave said. "She believes that jewel is evil."

"Nonsense," Colonel Musgrave muttered, tucking some papers into a folder. The top sheet read "Bank of London" and was stamped "LOAN PAST DUE."

"I'm afraid we'll have to speak with your guests to get to the bottom of this," Artie said.

"Of course," Colonel Musgrave said. "There aren't many people here, though. Most are due to arrive tomorrow."

"Who was in the house when the moon-stone disappeared?" Evan asked.

Colonel Musgrave stroked his mustache. "My wife and I were here. And my daughter,

Beatrice, who was the last to see the moonstone."

"Her groom, Richard Cunningham III, was on the third floor," Lady Musgrave said. "He agreed to stay up there. It's bad luck to see the bride before the wedding."

"Wealthy family, indeed," whispered Colonel Musgrave. His eyebrows wiggled up and down like two excited caterpillars.

"What about Kumar?" Cleo asked.

"Kumar is always here," said Colonel Musgrave.

"Was anyone else in the house?" Artie asked.

Colonel Musgrave thought for a moment. "Only Chef Lilith. She's been working in the kitchen."

"How many people know you keep the stone in the house?" Evan asked.

"Great Scott!" Colonel Musgrave said. "We don't keep the moonstone here. We keep it at the Bank of London!"

"We brought it out of the vault just for tomorrow's affair," Lady Musgrave said. "It was to be a surprise at the wedding."

"Unfortunately, we were the ones who were surprised," Colonel Musgrave said. He limped around the desk and leaned against it.

"So, the only people who knew the diamond was here are the people in this very house," Artie said.

Colonel Musgrave thought for a moment. "Just us and our banker, Jules Worthington IV. He dropped it off earlier today."

"Does everyone have a number after their name?" Cleo whispered to Evan.

"Are there any other items of value in the house?" Artie asked.

"Only our grandfather clock," the colonel said.

"It was a gift from the queen herself," Lady Musgrave said. "It's at the top of the stairs on the second floor."

"Splendid," Artie said. "If you don't mind, we'll start by questioning your daughter."

"Oh, can't you let her rest?" said Lady Musgrave. "She's ill and under great stress. Anyhow, Beatrice would never steal."

"That may be true," Artie said, "but we need to be thorough. She was the last one to see the moonstone."

"Very well," Colonel Musgrave said. "She's upstairs in her bedroom."

As Evan, Cleo, and Artie left the room, they bumped into a thin man wearing a silk top hat. He had the shiniest fingernails Evan had ever seen.

"You must be the detectives," the man said, shaking their hands. "I'm Jules Worthington, Colonel Musgrave's banker. The bank is eager to see the stone returned. Now, please excuse me, I must speak with Colonel Musgrave."

"I understand," Artie said. "However, we have some questions first."

Worthington pulled a gold pocket watch from his vest and glanced at it. "I don't have much time," he said, tapping his well-shined shoe on the marble floor.

"It'll only take a moment," Cleo said.

Worthington glanced at his watch again. "Of course," he said. "Anything to help."

"You were in charge of bringing the moonstone here?" Evan asked.

Worthington nodded. "Our security team delivered the stone in an iron lockbox. We

searched the house, gave the moonstone to Musgrave, and left. Then I returned to the bank. My secretary can tell you I didn't leave until I found out about the theft."

Evan jotted a few notes.

"What's the value of the moonstone?" Cleo asked.

"It's priceless," Worthington said.

"But let's say you were trying to sell it," Cleo said.

Worthington rubbed his chin. "It's insured for more than a million pounds."

Artie gasped.

Evan stopped scribbling in the journal.

Watson drooled.

"That's pretty heavy," Cleo said.

"Pounds are *dollars* in England," Evan said.

"Oh," Cleo said. "Then, that's a lot of money."

"Indeed," Worthington said. He glanced at his watch and then looked out the towering window. The moon still hung red in the sky. "Now, I must speak with Colonel Musgrave. It's urgent."

"Do you mind if we ask why?" Evan said.

"I'm going to insist on removing the grandfather clock from the house and securing it in our vault," Worthington said. "As long as this mystery remains unsolved, we must be careful. The security team will be here before midnight, and I will oversee the job myself. I'm sorry. This can't wait any longer."

Worthington pushed past them and disappeared into Musgrave's study.

CHAPTER 7

When they found her, Beatrice Musgrave was lying across her bed in her nightgown. She coughed into a lacy white handkerchief.

"I was planning to wear the moonstone in my wedding tiara tomorrow," she wailed. "Now the diamond is gone and I've come down with a case of the croup!"

She coughed again. Evan didn't think it sounded very serious.

"When was the last time you saw the moonstone?" Artie asked.

"Nearly two hours ago," she said. "I placed it on my pillow while I fetched some glue." She pointed to a bottle on the nightstand. Goopy golden liquid dripped down the side.

"Why'd you need glue?" Evan asked.

"How else could I attach the diamond to my tiara?" Beatrice said. "When I returned, the moonstone was gone!"

"Was anyone else here?" Cleo asked.

"Only me," Beatrice said.

Kumar entered holding a silver tray. "Your tea, Miss Beatrice."

"Thank you," Beatrice said.

"Kumar," Artie said. "Where were you when the stone disappeared?"

"In the kitchen stirring the soup with Chef Lilith." He held out his arms. "You can see it on my sleeves."

Beatrice poured cream into her tea. "Kumar didn't steal the moonstone," she said. "He's practically family."

"Someone stole it," Artie said. "Someone in this very house."

Beatrice coughed again and then leaned toward them. "I know who did it."

"Who?" Evan and Cleo said at once.

Beatrice held the back of her hand to her forehead. "I can't say!" she cried dramatically.

Watson quietly woofed at her.

"All right, all right! I'll tell you!" She held her handkerchief to her face. "Last week, I overheard a conversation. The person said getting his hands on that gem is the most important thing in his life!"

"Who said that?" demanded Artie. "Who stole the moonstone?"

Beatrice's hands were shaking so much her teacup rattled against her saucer.

"My fiancé stole the Musgrave Moonstone. It was Richard Cunningham III!"

Evan, Cleo, and Artie made their way toward the second-floor landing, where a stairway led to Cunningham's room. Gas lamps lit the hallway, and the deep blood-red moon filled the window at the top of the stairs.

"Oh, the grandfather clock," Cleo said. "Let's have a look."

At least eight feet high, the clock towered above them. The base was made of four carved stags whose antlers supported the case

above it. Behind a glass door hung gleaming chimes and a long brass pendulum that swung back and forth. Above that, a silver clock face stared out, as large as a pizza pan and encircled by gems of every color. At the top, a large red ruby glinted at the twelve o'clock mark.

"That's one fancy clock," Evan said.

Artie climbed on a chair and looked closely at the lowermost gem. "Fancy, but fake," he said.

"Fake?" Cleo said.

"We studied gemology in police training," Artie said. "Those stones may look lovely, but they aren't worth much."

They continued across the landing. The entry hall stretched below them. Their footsteps echoed on the floor.

"There sure are a whole lot of suspects," Evan said.

"And a lot of opportunity," Cleo added. "People have been running all over the house to get ready for the wedding."

Evan opened his journal. "There's Kumar, Beatrice, Cunningham, Chef Lilith, Lady Musgrave, and Colonel Musgrave himself."

"You don't think Colonel or Lady Musgrave would steal their own gem, do you?" Cleo said.

"You can never rule someone out until you can rule him or her out for sure," Artie said. "Worthington told us the gem was insured for over a million pounds. That means if we don't find the diamond, Musgrave gets the money."

"Colonel Musgrave has money problems," Evan said. "I saw past-due bills on his desk."

"But what about Cunningham?" Cleo said. "Beatrice said—"

"Let's speak to him before we draw conclusions," Artie said.

"And what about the banker?" Evan offered, adding Worthington to his list. "He knew the stone was here, too."

The chandelier above them jingled. Cleo looked up. Before she could say anything, it began to fall. She shoved Evan and Artie and dove out of the way. The chandelier missed them by inches, smashing on the floor. Shards of crystal flew everywhere.

Artie scrambled to investigate. The chandelier was a twisted wreck.

"That was close!" Evan said. "What are the chances a chandelier would drop right when we're walking under it?"

Artie examined the rope that had fastened it to the ceiling. "The chances were good," he said. "Someone cut this rope."

"Where's Watson?" Cleo asked worriedly.

They heard a woof from the far side of the hallway. Watson was sniffing at the bottom edge of a curtain. Artie pulled it aside to reveal a hook on the wall. A frayed rope hung from it.

"This is where the person cut the rope," Artie said. "They must have escaped out this open window."

They looked out. A narrow ledge wrapped around the building.

"Probably a good thing they're gone," Cleo said. "If they cut the rope, it means they're holding a knife."

She moved close to Evan. "Do you really think solving this crime will help us get out of this crazy book?" she whispered.

"There's only one way to find out," Evan said. "And remember Ms. Hilliard's letter.

Keep your eyes open for a key. And anything that might help us find her."

"One thing's for sure," Cleo said.

"What's that?" Evan said.

"You're doing a great job proving you're not *totally* fragile."

CHAPTER 8

Cleo pushed past Evan and Artie and boosted herself onto the windowsill.

"Where are you going?" Evan said. He glanced nervously at the narrow ledge. "Cunningham is on the third floor."

"The best way to figure out who stole the Musgrave Moonstone is to find out who tried to drop a giant chandelier on our heads," Cleo said. "We need to chase this clue while the trail is still hot."

"Hot," Artie said. "I like that."

Cleo shimmied out onto the ledge. "Let's go."

Artie scooped Watson under one arm. "Shall I go next?"

"I'm going *last*," Evan said.

Artie climbed onto the ledge and edged out.

Evan looked down. It was a long drop to the ground below.

Evan worried about his parents. How would they feel if he just disappeared? He and Cleo had been in *The Case of the Mysterious Moonstone* for a few hours already. Wouldn't someone have noticed they were gone? He must have missed math class and trombone lessons by now. He knew if they didn't solve the crime and find some special key, they'd be trapped in this book forever. But falling from a second-story ledge seemed much, much worse.

Then he thought about Ms. Hilliard. She was trapped in a book, too. He needed to help her. She was the best librarian ever. She was smart and funny, and never pressured Evan to "go outside and get some fresh air." If he didn't help Ms. Hilliard escape, who would? Evan pulled himself onto the windowsill and crawled out into the blood-red night.

Even though the moon looked creepy, Evan was glad it was up there lighting his way. He crawled along the ledge behind Cleo and Artie. His heart thumped in his chest. His fingers curled tight around a gargoyle head.

"One inch at a time," he whispered to himself. "One inch at a time."

"Hey," Cleo called back. "There's a rope ladder over here!"

"Does it go up or down?" Artie asked, shifting Watson to his other arm.

"Both," she said. "It's hanging from a third-floor window and reaches to the ground."

Evan crept over to have a look. Two thick ropes dangled down the length of the house. Wooden rungs stretched between them, spaced around a foot apart.

"We have no way of knowing which way our mystery person went," Artie said.

Watson woofed.

"Not so fast," Evan said. "Look there. Another clue!"

On the end of one of the rungs, a small piece of white fabric flapped in the breeze.

"It must have torn off the mystery person's

clothing when he or she was trying to escape," Evan said.

"Too bad Watson isn't a bloodhound," Cleo said. "He'd sniff that fabric and lead us right to the thief."

Artie smiled. "Watson is full of surprises . . . Watch . . ."

Artie brought the piece of cloth close to Watson's nose. The dog sniffed the fabric and began wagging his tail.

"Which way did the scoundrel go?" Artie said.

Watson looked up and down. A long string of drool dripped out of his mouth and landed on the rung below the ledge.

"Well, that did us no good," Cleo said.

"Oh no?" Artie said. "What's that?" He pointed at the drool on the ladder.

"It's saliva," Evan said. "Spit. Drool. Glistening slobber."

"It's gross," Cleo said.

"Remember the first rule of detective work," Artie said. "Always follow the slobber."

And with that, Artie stuffed Watson into his coat, grabbed the rope ladder, and began climbing down.

Once Artie reached the bottom, Cleo followed. The rope ladder didn't look strong enough to support more than one of them at a time. Evan waited for Cleo to get her feet on the ground and took hold of the ladder himself.

The rope ladder swayed with each step, but Evan thought a ladder—even a wobbly one—seemed safer than a narrow ledge. He swung back and forth. Evan's knuckles scraped across the stone. His fingers stung.

"Hey," Evan called down. "What do you get when you cross a detective with a cashew?"

"Now's not the time for a joke," Cleo said.

"Jokes help me relax," Evan said.

When he reached the ground, Evan looked at his hands. He had scrapes across three fingers on his right hand.

"Oww!" Cleo said, sucking on one of her knuckles. "That stone is rougher than it looks."

Artie held up his hand to reveal a long scrape from his fingers to his wrist. "We match. Now, let's hurry before the trail gets cold."

They followed a stone path around the back of the house.

"So what *do* you get when you cross a detective with a cashew?" Artie asked as they passed through a gate.

"A nut case," Evan said.

"Ha, I get it," Artie said.

Watson lifted his head and began to snuffle.

"Something's cooking," Evan said. "We must be near the kitchen."

They crept to an open window. Just inside, a huge pot of tomato soup bubbled. A wooden spoon the size of a baseball bat stuck out of it. A woman was bent over the countertop with her back to them. She wore a white apron tied around her waist and a tall white hat.

"That must be Chef Lilith," whispered Cleo.

"She's wearing white," Artie said. "And look . . ."

He pointed to her apron. The corner was torn off.

"Just like the strip of cloth we found," Evan said.

Cleo began climbing through the window. "Well, that solves it," she said.

But Evan noticed something else. Her shoes had the pointiest toes and the highest heels he had ever seen. "Wait!" he whispered. He tried to grab Cleo, but she was soccer goalie fast.

Cleo scurried through the open window, marched across the kitchen, and cleared her throat. "You're under arrest, Chef Lilith. Drop your tomato and turn around."

The woman slowly turned. It was their mean librarian, Ms. Crowley.

And she wasn't holding a tomato.

She was holding a knife.

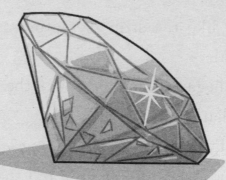

CHAPTER 9

Artie leaped through the window. "London Police!" he cried out. "Drop the knife!"

"Good heavens," Ms. Crowley said. "I was only cutting vegetables." She pointed at the counter where piles of carrots, onions, and potatoes sat. "So much to do for this wedding, you know."

"Ms. Crowley," Cleo said. "It's us. Cleo and Evan."

Evan stumbled through the open window.

"Pleasure to meet you," she said, "but I'm not sure who this Ms. Crowley is. My name is Chef Lilith Merriweather. I studied cooking in Paris and have been working for the finest families in England for many years."

"But you're . . . you're . . ." Evan said.

"I am *Chef Lilith*," the woman said again, "not this Ms. Crowley you are speaking of. I would appreciate it if my junior Frank Hardy and Nancy Drew would stop mistaking me for someone I am clearly not."

She was smiling, but her glare was unmistakable. It was Ms. Crowley for sure.

"My friends must be confused," Artie said. "I've read about you in the *Gazette*. You once prepared a feast for Queen Victoria."

"And a magnificent feast it was," Chef Lilith said. "Roasted quail, cod in oyster sauce, and Cumberland duck."

"Sounds delightful," Artie said.

"Sounds like a stomachache," mumbled Evan.

"If you don't mind, may we ask you a few questions?" Artie said.

Chef Lilith crossed her arms. "You may," she said.

Evan was weirded out. Ms. Crowley was somehow inside this book with them, but she didn't want anyone to know who she was. Why? He guessed he needed to play along to find out. "Where were you when the moonstone disappeared?" he asked.

"I was here in the kitchen with Kumar," she said.

Watson woofed.

"Why did you cut that rope and drop a chandelier on our heads?" Cleo asked.

"What?" Chef Lilith said. "I would never do such a thing, but I did notice a knife missing from my cutting block."

Artie grabbed the huge spoon and stirred the soup. "This smells delightful."

"It's my specialty," Chef Lilith said. "Tomato soup with garlic and basil. Beatrice insisted it be served at the wedding."

"I'm curious," Artie said, lifting the spoon from the pot. "Are fake rubies an ingredient in your recipe?"

He dumped out the spoon. A red stone clattered across the countertop.

"How do you know it's fake?" Cleo asked.

"Fake gemstones float," Artie said. "Real ones sink."

"Someone has tampered with my soup!" Chef Lilith cried out.

"You've torn your apron," Evan said. "Do you mind if we have a look?"

Chef Lilith bunched up her apron and turned away. "I'm very busy."

"It'll only take a moment," Artie said. He took the piece of white cloth they had found on the rope ladder and held it to the torn edge of the apron.

It didn't fit. The bit of cloth was too large.

"Satisfied?" Chef Lilith said. "Now, please excuse me, I've got to fetch eggs for the soufflé. Perhaps Evan and Cleo could help me."

"Of course," Artie said. "I'll just have a look around the kitchen."

Behind the house, Ms. Crowley led the kids down a dark path to the chicken coop. They

heard rustling on the roosts. A cluster of chickens slept in the light of the red moon.

Ms. Crowley began rooting around the nesting boxes. She came out with a handful of eggs and placed them into Cleo's gathered dress.

"I'm not sure how you two got here, but you've got to stay in character," she said. "If you raise suspicion that you're not who you say you are, the whole investigation will be over. Artie Baker will be fired and all three of us will be stuck in this book forever." Ms. Crowley began loading Evan's pockets with eggs. "As far as anyone knows, I'm Chef Lilith and you two are assistants to that bumbling detective and his drooling pooch. Understand?"

Evan and Cleo nodded.

"If you got into this world just before us, how did Artie hear of Chef Lilith?" Cleo asked.

"This is fiction," Ms. Crowley said. "We are characters in that fiction, and all characters have backstories. We have to play along."

"This fiction feels pretty real," Cleo said.

"And the stakes are high," Ms. Crowley said.

"You really didn't know about that fake ruby in the soup?" Evan asked.

"No," Ms. Crowley said. "It's probably a clue. Or a red herring."

"Why is there fish in tomato soup?" Cleo asked.

"Not a fish," Ms. Crowley said. "A red herring is a false clue. They show up in mysteries all the time."

"How do you know so much about cooking?" Evan asked. "You're a librarian."

"I watch a lot of cooking shows. Mostly, I'm faking it. I hope you're doing the same."

"What if we enter a book and we're pilots or racecar drivers or astronauts?" Evan asked.

Ms. Crowley filled a basket with the remaining eggs and locked the chicken coop. "Then, you'd better learn quickly," she said. "Now, get back inside and interview your next suspect."

"I think we should go see Richard Cunningham," Evan said.

CHAPTER 10

"Mr. Cunningham," Artie said, pacing across the third-floor bedroom. "Where were you when the moonstone disappeared?"

Richard Cunningham III turned to face them from the armchair near the window. The belt of his velvet robe struggled to stay tied over his round belly.

"I've been in my room the whole time," Cunningham said, pulling his tea tray closer.

"How did you meet Beatrice?" Cleo asked.

"We only met face-to-face two months ago," Cunningham said. "Three years before that, her parents suggested we meet and I sent her a letter from South Africa. I fell in love with her after her first response. Such perfect handwriting! The loops on her Gs are magical. When I finally convinced her to wed, she insisted on this date for the wedding."

"Who else has been up here?" Evan asked.

Cunningham thought a moment. "Other than the team from the bank and the police, only Colonel Musgrave," he said. "He came to discuss our merger."

Watson woofed.

"What merger?" Artie asked.

Cunningham sipped his tea. "My family's shipping company in South Africa will be merging with Colonel Musgrave's in India. Our two companies will be one."

"Who stands to benefit from this merger?" Artie asked.

"Both sides," Cunningham said. "Musgrave's routes in India are risky, too many pirates. Our company needs more influence with the queen. Merging will help us both."

"And how are you at climbing rope ladders?" Artie asked.

"Rope ladders?" Cunningham said. "What sort of question is that?"

Artie reached out the window and began pulling the ladder into the room. "There happens to be one hanging from your window."

"I had no idea!" Cunningham stood and smoothed out his robe. "Anyhow, that ladder would never support my weight."

Evan tugged at the ladder. It felt flimsy.

"What do you know about the Musgrave Moonstone?" Cleo said, narrowing her eyes.

Cunningham smiled. "It's one of the finest stones ever unearthed."

"And stealing the Musgrave Moonstone—" Artie started.

"Stealing the Musgrave Moonstone would do me no good," Cunningham said. "Our companies will be merging. I'll be marrying Musgrave's daughter. The stone was going to be mine anyway. Now if you'll excuse me, I must speak with Musgrave."

Cunningham stuffed his pudgy feet into his slippers and marched out.

"Solving this crime is not gonna be simple," Cleo said.

Artie straightened his tie. "It's a complex mystery," he said. "So, the solution must be complicated."

"We've got too many suspects," Evan said as they went down to the second floor. A railing overlooked the entrance hall.

"And anyone could have snuck away to grab that moonstone," Cleo said.

"Maybe we should go over what we've found," Evan suggested.

They sat at a small table near the giant grandfather clock. The gem-covered clock face sparkled in the eerie moonlight. Artie pulled out some dog treats and placed them beside Watson on a velvet chair. Evan opened his journal to see what he had written . . .

SUSPECTS:

COLONEL MUSGRAVE
- Motive: Money troubles, insurance policy for over 1 million pounds!
- Alibi: With Lady Musgrave

LADY MUSGRAVE
- Motive: Believes the stone is cursed. Wants to get rid of it.
- Alibi: With Colonel Musgrave

BEATRICE

BEATRICE'S TEARS →

- Motive: Last person to see the diamond. Could she have lost it?
- Alibi: She says she was in the hall getting glue

RICHARD CUNNINGHAM III
- Motive: Was heard saying he wants "that gem."

CUNNINGHAM'S SPILLED TEA

- **Alibi**: Alone in his room the whole time

WATSON'S DROOL →

KUMAR

- **Motive**: None. He says he is loyal to the family.
- **Alibi**: In the kitchen with Chef Lilith

CHEF LILITH

- **Motive**: Money? Plus, she's creepy and mean.

TOMATO SOUP →

- **Alibi**: Cooking all afternoon, Kumar can confirm

JULES WORTHINGTON IV

- **Motive**: Maybe money? He knows how much the stone is worth.
- **Alibi**: At the bank when the moonstone disappeared

"I don't see any clues that tell us who did it," Cleo said.

"We've got to dig deeper," Artie said. "The answer is here somewhere."

Suddenly, Evan heard a clatter above them. A tea cart came hurtling down the staircase, right for them.

"Watch out!" he cried.

Cleo and Artie rolled out of the way. But Watson sat on his cushioned chair munching on his treats. Evan dove in front of the tea cart and scooped him up. Then Evan leaped out of the way right before the heavy metal cart came crashing down. The tray flipped into the air. The teapot and teacups shattered on the floor. When the dust settled, the velvet chair was splintered and there was a huge tea-cart-sized hole in the wall.

"That . . . that could have been us," Cleo said.

"But it was fortuitous!" Artie exclaimed.

Cleo looked at Evan so he could tell her what "fortuitous" meant, but not even Evan knew.

"It means 'filled with fortune or good luck,'" Artie said.

"What's fortuitous about a giant tea cart almost crushing us?" Evan said.

"It means our thief is still in the house." Artie dusted himself off and stood up. "And I know who did it."

CHAPTER 11

Artie paced up and down the hallway. The grandfather clock read 11:54 and everyone was there: Colonel and Lady Musgrave, Kumar, Beatrice, Cunningham, Chef Lilith, and Worthington.

"Oh dear, now the groom has seen the bride," Lady Musgrave said. "More bad luck for the Musgrave family!"

"Mother, the wedding is not until tomorrow." Beatrice sighed.

"I hope this will be quick," Worthington said. He glanced at his watch, which he held in a gloved hand. "My men will be here soon to remove the grandfather clock for safekeeping."

"If we catch the thief, we won't need your men," Evan said.

"*If*," Cleo said. "I don't see how our clues add up to anything."

"Please, everyone, let Detective Baker speak," Musgrave said. He sat on a leather chair and crossed his good leg over his wooden one.

"At first, I was stumped," Artie said, walking past each suspect as he spoke. "Although you were all in the house, none of you had the opportunity to steal the moonstone. It was with Beatrice the whole time."

"Except when I left the room to get the glue," Beatrice said.

"Precisely," Artie said. "This puzzled me until I realized that trying to discover who came into Beatrice's bedroom might not be the best place to start."

"Get to the point," Musgrave bellowed.

"We know our thief tried to crush us with the chandelier and used the rope ladder hanging from the third floor to move secretly around the house," Artie said. "If we can figure out who used that ladder, we'll know who committed the crime."

"Anyone could have used it," Chef Lilith said.

"Not just anyone," Evan said. "Colonel Musgrave has a wooden leg. He could never step on the rungs."

"And Lady Musgrave's poofy skirts would have gotten in the way," Cleo said.

Artie looked Cunningham up and down. "Cunningham, you're way too heavy to have used the ladder," he said.

"I'm not *that* heavy," Cunningham said, sucking in his belly. "But in this case, I'm glad to be carrying a few extra pounds."

"And by that you don't mean British money, right?" Cleo said. She bent down and scratched Watson behind the ears.

"We saw Beatrice and Kumar in Beatrice's room just before the chandelier fell on us, so we know neither of them could have cut the rope," Evan said.

Artie strode across the carpeted hallway and stood in front of Worthington. "That leaves just one person," Artie said.

Worthington took a tiny step back. "What are you suggesting?" he asked.

"I'm not *suggesting* anything," Artie said. I'm *saying* that Jules Worthington IV stole the Musgrave Moonstone!"

"Preposterous!" Worthington said. "I have witnesses to prove I was at the bank when the moonstone disappeared."

Artie sighed. "And that's where I'm stumped," he said.

"You can't go around accusing people of crimes," Worthington said. "Now, if you'll excuse me, I need to meet my men downstairs so they can move the clock."

Evan felt the sting from the scrape on his right hand, and that gave him an idea. "What if I can prove you were on that rope ladder?" he said.

"You couldn't possibly . . ." Worthington said.

"Why are you wearing gloves?" Evan asked.

"It's a bit chilly tonight," Worthington said shiftily.

"No, it's not," Kumar said, stepping around the smashed chandelier. "It's warmer than Rajasthan in late August."

"I noticed Worthington's shiny fingernails when we first met him," Evan said. "Now he's wearing gloves. We scraped our hands climbing down the rope ladder. I'll bet Worthington did, too."

"Worthington was with the bank team when they searched the house," Cleo said. "He could have attached the rope ladder to the windowsill then."

"Worthington, remove your gloves," Colonel Musgrave said.

Worthington glared at Musgrave and then peeled off his gloves. A large scrape stretched from his wrist to his knuckles. "This doesn't prove anything," he said. "I could have gotten this scrape anywhere. Without the diamond, without proving how it was stolen, you have no case. Now, I must insist—"

"I must insist you stay right where you are," Evan said. He walked across the hallway and stood in front of the huge grandfather clock. "I know where the Musgrave Moonstone has been hiding all along!"

CHAPTER 12

Evan climbed on a chair and swung open the glass covering the clock face. It was almost midnight, and the colored gems marking each hour sparkled in the moonlight.

"None of those are the Musgrave Moonstone," Lady Musgrave said. "Those gems are all colored: red, yellow, blue, green, and purple!"

"Colonel Musgrave said the moonstone changes depending on the phase of the moon,"

Evan said. "It glows bright white when the moon is full and turns gray, almost black, when there's no moon."

"What does that prove?" Cunningham asked.

"Tonight is the blood moon," Evan said. "If the stories about the diamond are true, it should have turned red tonight, at least until the blood moon ends."

Artie looked at the clock. "And that should be right about now," he said.

The chimes inside the grandfather clock began to toll. Twelve bells for midnight.

Through the window, the deep red of the blood moon faded to a pale orange and, soon after, to white.

The bright red stone that sat over the twelve on the clock face changed, too, from a deep red, to pale orange, to brilliant white.

"The moonstone!" Colonel Musgrave cried out.

"I have the gem from the clock right here," Artie said, pulling it from his pocket. "It was floating in Chef Lilith's soup."

"Then Chef Lilith stole the moonstone!" Worthington said. "I was at the bank! I have witnesses!"

"That's what's tough about this crime," Cleo said. "It's a complex mystery."

Artie perked up. "So, the solution must be complicated!" he said. "Of course! There were *two* people involved!"

Everyone began looking at one another.

"Well, who was it?" Lady Musgrave said, placing a hand on her husband's shoulder.

Cleo winked at Evan. "You may not be as fragile as you seem," she whispered, "but I'm also not as dim."

"I never said you were dim," Evan said.

"Out with it," Colonel Musgrave said. "Who did it?"

Cleo looked down the line of suspects. "The person who helped steal the Musgrave Moonstone was Beatrice Musgrave!"

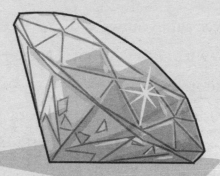

CHAPTER 13

"I—I did no such thing!" Beatrice shrieked. She placed the back of her hand on her forehead, lay down across a long sofa, and fanned herself with her handkerchief.

"There," Cleo said, pointing at the clock. "It's the same glue you had in your bedroom. I can see it around the edge of the diamond." She grabbed a spoon from the broken tea set, climbed up next to Evan, and carefully pried the gemstone from the face of the clock. "You

left your room at eight, replaced the stone on the clock with the Musgrave Moonstone, and used the ladder to climb down to the kitchen. Your handkerchief protected your hand from getting scraped. Once there, you dropped the stone from the clock into the soup."

"You insisted on Chef Lilith's famous tomato soup for your wedding," Evan said. "That's because it's hard to see a red stone in red soup!"

"Tomato, garlic, and basil soup," Chef Lilith corrected him, holding up her giant spoon. "It's famous."

"Your plan might have worked if you knew more about fake gems," Artie said. "Fake gems float."

"It was Richard!" Beatrice said. "I heard him say that acquiring the gem is the most important thing in his life!"

"I was speaking to your father about you, my little emerald!" Cunningham said.

"This is too much for me to handle!" Beatrice cried. "I'm too fragile!"

Cleo and Evan hopped down.

Colonel Musgrave crossed the hallway and took his daughter's hand. "Dearest Beatrice," he said. "Is it true? Did you plan this theft?"

Cunningham dropped to his knee beside Beatrice. "Were you never planning to marry me, my fluffy monkey?" he asked.

"You look nothing like the photograph you sent," Beatrice said. "Anyhow, we both know this marriage is more about my father's company than about me. Plus, the mosquitoes in South Africa are larger than house cats!" Beatrice began to weep into her handkerchief.

Evan noticed a piece of it was torn off.

"Look," Evan said. He held up the scrap of fabric they had found on the rope ladder. "It's a perfect fit."

"It was Worthington's idea!" Beatrice cried. "He said no one would be hurt. He said the insurance company would pay Daddy for the lost diamond and we would sell the moonstone and be happy together!"

"This is absurd," Worthington said, sneering. "The worst detective on the London police force and two brats figuring out my plans? I was supposed to be on my way to America by now!"

"*America?*" Beatrice wailed. "You told me to meet you on the ship to *Italy*!"

Worthington's face twitched. "Plans change, bunny." He lunged across the hallway and snatched the Musgrave Moonstone

from Cleo. Worthington turned to run, but Watson snapped his teeth onto the banker's pants and snarled. Evan and Cleo grabbed hold of his arms. But Worthington pulled free of them all.

Whack!

That's when Chef Lilith conked him on the head with her giant spoon.

Worthington dropped to the floor, dazed. One boat ticket to America fell from his pocket.

Kumar clutched Worthington's jacket. "The only trip you'll be taking is to jail," he said.

"I've always wanted to say that," Artie said, disappointed.

"Feel free," Kumar said.

Artie turned to Worthington and opened his mouth to speak. He exhaled. "Well, now you've taken all the fun out of it," he said.

"Why don't you find the fun in putting on the handcuffs?" Evan said.

"Grand idea!" Artie said. He pulled out a set of iron handcuffs and snapped them on Worthington's wrists. "The only banking you'll be doing . . ." Artie paused. "Is banking . . . in jail."

"That made no sense," Evan said.

"Yes, I'll have to work on that," Artie said. "In the meantime, I'll send word to Chief Rutherford that this crime has been solved."

Watson woofed.

Cleo clapped. "Your job is saved!" she said.

"It looks that way." Artie began emptying his pockets. He pulled out a sealed purple envelope and handed it to Cleo. "Give me a moment while I find the key to the handcuffs."

The key. Evan and Cleo glanced at each other.

After loading most of a table with loose change, scraps of paper, and dog treats, Artie finally pulled out a thin chain. A silver key with swirling designs dangled from it. He held it out to the kids.

"Hold this for me," Artie said. "I don't want to lose it."

"Do you mind if I hold it as well?" Chef Lilith said. "I've always been interested in police work."

"Certainly," Artie said.

Evan, Cleo, and Chef Lilith grabbed the chain. Letters burst from the key like a thousand crazy spiders. The letters tumbled in the air around them and began to spell words. The words became sentences, the sentences paragraphs. Before long, they could barely see. And then everything went black.

CHAPTER 14

"Wake up," Ms. Crowley snapped.

Evan opened his eyes and lifted his head from the table. Cleo was sitting across from him. She must have dozed off, too. Plain wooden shelves surrounded them. The poster explaining the Dewey decimal system hung on the wall behind the checkout desk. They were back in their school library. Evan glanced at the clock. Only five minutes had passed.

Ms. Crowley loomed over them. "You're here to do your work, not to nap," she barked. "Now, gather your things. Recess is over."

Evan wiped a string of drool from his cheek.

"You're . . . you're not wearing that crazy suit," Cleo said to him.

"You remember that?" Evan said.

Cleo leaned across the table to whisper, "Two people can't be in the same dream, can they?"

"I don't think so," Evan said.

The bell rang.

"Go." Ms. Crowley began to tap her foot. "I have a kindergarten read-aloud in five minutes."

Evan slung his backpack onto his shoulders. "Ms. Crowley, do you like watching cooking shows on television?"

"Stop talking nonsense," Ms. Crowley said. "And stop burying your nose in all those books. They'll rot your brain."

But as they passed her into the hallway, Evan could swear he smelled tomato soup.

Kids began to fill the hallways as they came in from the playground.

"What do we do now?" Cleo asked. "Do we go on as though we didn't just solve a major crime?"

"I'm not sure," Evan said.

He felt a lump in his pocket. He reached in and pulled out a thin chain. A small silver key hung from it.

Evan's eyes brightened and he showed the key to Cleo.

Cleo patted her pockets and pulled out a purple envelope. She tore it open.

Evan, if you're reading this letter, I'm proud of you. In my last note, I warned you that you were too fragile, but only someone who loves stories as you do would have found the Lost Library.

I know telling you to go no further would be a waste of time, but please use caution. I hope you've brought a friend along. The Case of the Mysterious Moonstone is nothing compared to the challenges to come.

I'm not sure which librarian took my place at school, but not all of them are kind. Some may try to use the Lost Library for evil. Be wary.

Your friend
and librarian,
Ms. Sandie Hilliard

"If it didn't happen to me, I'd never believe it," Evan said.

"It did happen to us, and I still don't believe it!" Cleo said.

They walked down the hallway toward their next class. "I do know one thing," Evan said.

"What?" Cleo asked.

"I'm going back to the library tomorrow," he said. "We need to find Ms. Hilliard and stop Ms. Crowley from whatever she's up to."

Cleo grinned. "See you there, Sherlock!"

ABOUT THE AUTHOR

Eric Luper has written books for kids of all ages. He loves excitement and is always looking for his next adventure. Eric has fibbed his way into a tour of the ultra-secret PEZ headquarters, rebuilt a castle in France, explored the tunnels under Paris and Istanbul, escaped hungry crocodiles in Costa Rica, and rafted down the Colorado River. He lives with his family in Albany, New York.

NEVER LEAVE A BUG BEHIND—COLLECT ALL THE BATTLE BUGS BOOKS!